HAUNTING JOY

A.L. HAWKE

PHANTOM HEART, LLC

ISBN: 978-1-953919-80-9 Paperback

ISBN: 978-1-953919-78-6 Hardcover

ISBN: 978-1-953919-77-9 ebook

Library of Congress Control Number: 2025904524

Line edited by Stephanie Marshall Ward

Proofread by Alexa B.

Cover Design © 2025 by Mirella Santana

Published by Phantom Heart, LLC

27702 Crown Valley Pkwy, Suite D4 #201

Ladera Ranch, CA 92694

Printed and bound in the United States of America

First printing March, 2025

Learn more about A.L. Hawke at www.alhawke.com

Correspondence: contact@alhawke.com

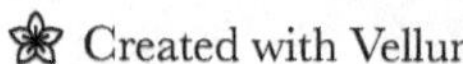 Created with Vellum

For my wife
My source and inspiration for joy

PLYMOUTH CREST

ALEC FELT A LIGHTER STEP TO HIS STRIDE THAT HE HARDLY recognized—it was not the cadence of his stride that felt new, but the feeling that went with it, deep inside. A feeling in his chest that he hadn't felt in such a long, long time. As he walked up the narrow path on the woodsy hillside, the tree trunks surrounded in lovely green thrush, he cherished this sensation. Chip, his best friend and realtor, walked beside him. Despite wearing a pressed navy-blue suit and carrying a leather briefcase, Chip seemed relaxed too. Because they knew what this feeling was all about. After months of searching, they had finally found the house.

The façade of the large structure had wood siding, painted white, and grand glass cottage windows. An ultra-modern roof was constructed at a single slope. Between big windows were assorted black and gray granite stones. And a concrete path, meandering amid leaves and bushes and more towering, thick-trunked trees, rose from the large dirt driveway. Weeds grew through the cracks in the pavement, particularly in the steps leading to the front door. The house was old. No matter. This was the same dream house he had seen in pictures on his computer. Here under the glistening bright sunrays, it felt so inviting. And looking back over his shoulder, he had the perfect view of the lake down the woodsy hillside.

Chip jostled keys by the front door.

"It was built in the nineties," Chip said with a shrug. "I know you wanted something new, Alec, but this is a very modern home, ahead of its time—despite the window frames. Windows are everywhere, and you told me how important that open feeling was to you. Honestly, the builder seemed to have the same taste as you. You could always remodel the windows and replace all the walls with glass, I suppose."

"It's all wonderful. Exactly as I pictured it."

"Yeah, well," Chip said with a chuckle, opening the door, "wait till you see inside, man."

"You said the owner was a filmmaker?"

"The original owner. He was some producer, or Hollywood agent, or something like that. Richer than *sh*…well you know. He had to be to build this mansion. But no one has lived in the house for years."

"You can say *richer than shit* to me, Chip."

"Not today, man," he said, hitting Alec's shoulder. "Today I'm your realtor."

"But I found the listing."

Chip frowned. But then he managed to regain his smile as he opened the door. He turned on a light switch and then gestured with a sweeping arm. They stood together in awe, gawking. The polished alabaster stone flooring blended into white carpet, heralding the true masterpiece of the house: a super spacious central living room. Alec ran his fingers through his dark beard, shaking his head. It was devoid of furniture, making an already expansive area seem huge.

Alec walked into the living room and gazed up. Here, an

indoor balcony circled around upstairs. It was a grand design he had seen in hotels and restaurants, but never in a home. The effect in this central room with a tall, vaulted ceiling over an indoor balcony was one of elegance and opulence, something very different from the surrounding forest. But the strangest thing was that, though it was evidently designed to feel open, groups of maple trees with thick trunks and full green foliage came close to the windows, creating a confined feeling. But that was wonderful too, because it made the home feel cozy. He could already imagine starting up the central fireplace, sipping some tea, and writing as it snowed outside.

"Large enough for a party," Alec quipped.

"That's the last thing I thought you'd say," Chip said with a laugh. "I thought you were looking for peace and quiet?"

"Just saying."

"Too bad it wasn't available back in the days, huh, Alec?"

Alec nodded. He took a deep breath and shook his head. A cold gust blew across his cheek from the still-open door, but something felt a little strange about it. For some reason, when he turned, he almost expected to see someone standing by the door watching them.

"Come on," Chip said. "Let me show you around. You've gotta see the kitchen. It looks brand new, immaculate, like it was hardly ever used."

"It's better than this?"

"Look, you can just sign the papers now if you want to," Chip quipped with a laugh. "Don't act so desperate, man. We still have to get you a good deal."

"How come everything is so clean? You said it's been unoccupied for years? I hardly see any dust."

"The owner's probably been looking over the place from time to time. All the old ratty furniture was recently sold, I hear. They probably cleaned the place up for us for the sale. It's an investment."

Alec followed Chip across the living room, under the mezzanine, and into a kitchen. The kitchen was empty, but there were silver stoves and ovens with a large central island. Expensive looking appliances, of course—no doubt the reason his friend wanted to show him.

"Viking stoves," Chip said. "Stainless steel ovens. Subzero fridge. Not sure it'll do much for your bachelorself, but it's pretty top rate."

"My daughter cooks. She can use all of this when she visits. As long as I have a toaster, I can make do." Then Alec shook his head. "Wow. But…yeah, this kitchen doesn't look used at all. None of the place looks like it was ever used."

"I'm thinking it was constructed and then forgotten. You know, there's not many *yous* looking to live in the middle of nowhere—like totally in the middle of nowhere, man. When was the last time we saw someone on the road? If quiet is what you were asking for, this is the place. Come on. I got one more thing to show you that will blow your mind. Wait till you see this. When I saw it, all I was thinking is that this is what you were asking for in your early retirement home, you old fart."

"I'm the same age as you, Chip."

"Sure, well, some of us ain't lucky enough to enjoy retirement before fifty."

As they walked across the second-story balcony, Alec ran his hand along the wooden rail. Again, no dust. That was unsettling. Despite no furniture, the place looked like it was in pristine condition. Sure, Chip had said it was probably cleaned up after the furniture was moved, but Chip had also told Alec that it was cleaned out over nine months ago. Everything in the home was totally immaculate, a mystery his best friend, an all-too-inexperienced realtor, wasn't too concerned about. No, his friend seemed way too excited to really be concerned about anything.

As they approached the stairs, Alec felt another chill in the air. The source seemed to be the front door, but now the door was closed.

There was a Spanish feel to the hallways. It wasn't just the indoor balcony, the hallways were arched. Still, all the walls were painted colonial white.

They walked around the upstairs floor as Alec gazed down at the expansive room below. Then they surveyed four bedrooms and two bathrooms that felt extraordinarily ordinary. There was nothing wrong with that. The rooms were large with decent closets and, again, all were very clean.

"Enough of the small stuff," Chip said. "You have got to see this."

Alec followed Chip past a glass window overlooking the woodsy outdoors, and then into the largest room in the house. This was the master bedroom, spanning the entire front of the home. It was a huge room with a fireplace, a small sunken section in a corner, and, of course, walled by windows. But Chip ignored all of that, walking straight across the room to a glass door.

Alec trailed his friend outside onto a very large cement terrace. The outdoor balcony was similar to the indoor, spanning the front yard and then continuing over the side yard. It was spacious and very wide, but also a little unnerving with only a shallow wall separating a ledge from a sheer drop down the hillside. The side yard, to his right, was full of more trees surrounding a small cement patio. But it was the overlook in the front that his friend had, no doubt, wanted him to see. Far down the woodsy hillside was a gorgeous view of the lake. And now, with clear skies, yellow light sparkled golden on the large body of water.

Alec took a deep breath, taking in the fresh nutty and

woodsy scent of the surrounding maple trees. He gazed up, and a hawk hovered amongst wisps of white clouds in an otherwise clear azure sky. He followed the large bird as it swooped down, passing over the green foliage. Then he lost the bird in the trees near the shore.

He was surprised to spot a stranger standing by the water. She wore a draping black shawl that hung down almost to her feet. The lady crouched down on her knees by the water, seemingly staring down at her own reflection. When she rose, she picked up a stone and tossed it into the water. Then she just cradled herself in her arms, looking out at the lake, seemingly in as much wonder as he was.

"So, what'dya think?"

"Huh?" Alec whirled around. "Oh. Yeah." He nodded to his friend, who stood near the short cement wall, admiring the lake too.

"Figured you could write here," Chip said.

"I bet you did," Alec said with a laugh. "So…what's the catch?"

"Well, it's the most expensive place I've shown you. And you asked for a place in the woods, but not this far from town. This is very, very, very far from nowhere. There's just a gas station and store along the road. That's about a five-minute drive down the hill. Your hill. The closest real town around here is called Badger. We drove past Badger too. I doubt you noticed. It was like two blocks long and is about twenty minutes south of here. I caught a few buildings and a Walmart. Not much else. So, I guess, if you don't mind stocking up and truly living like a hermit in frigid snow, this place should suit you fine."

"What's the deal with the place being vacant for so many years?"

"I don't know, but I wouldn't worry. If you like the place, its past vacancy shouldn't be a problem. Take it as an added bonus. Nobody lives here, Alec. Nobody. That's why it's priced so low, I figure."

"It's the best place we've seen. But a bit too nice and affordable."

"You're always suspicious. Don't worry, man. I'll dot the i's and cross the t's before we enter escrow. That is…*if* you want me to start escrow?"

"I'll take it," Alec said. But then he shook his head. "If the seller keeps the asking price. I can't afford what this place is probably really worth. I love it, but…something feels off. Maybe it's too good to be true?"

"Because you always worry," Chip said with a larger grin. Then he put an arm on his shoulder. "I'll get you the deal, maybe even slash a bit off the selling price. You wanted a place to rest by a lake. Right? To write? Even added a nice view, didn't I? Well, voilà, your Shangri-la awaits, sir."

"I found the place, Chip."

Chip lost his smile.

"Of course, I love it," Alec said with a chuckle, hitting his friend's shoulder. "Make the deal and I'm in."

Chip regained his grin. Then he gazed back out at the view, shaking his head.

Alec felt a cold breeze brush over his shoulder again. It seemed to be coming from the lake. The stranger far below in her shawl was still kneeling over the water. It was like she was still gazing at her own reflection, and under the sunlight reflected off the lake, her whole body seemed to shimmer.

"It sure is a nice view," said Chip.

Alec smirked at his friend. But then he startled when he gazed back down. The lady by the lake had disappeared.

IT WAS PRETTY ENOUGH GREEN

ALEC SPENT HIS FIRST DAY WALKING DOWN THE HILLSIDE, skidding this way and that over leaves and mud, around thick tree trunks, all the way down until he landed by a two-lane road. Although the leaves were everywhere, the trees were sparse enough for him to move around them and use the trunks as breaks in his descent. And he hadn't been the first to do this. There were lines and gaps between the bushes likely made by prior hikers. His descent took about forty minutes. He could have made it down a lot faster—maybe in twenty—walking down a larger manmade trail, but he preferred taking his time scaling down the less trodden paths.

The lake was across the two-lane road by the base of the hill. But Alec wasn't heading to the lake, he wanted to visit Plymouth Hill. Beside him, along the road, a sign read "Plymouth Hill, two miles." No matter, he'd enjoy continuing to walk.

What a walk it was. There was that wonderful maple tree scent. And so little noise. Not a car passed. That was probably because the only turn toward the main road ended at the top of the hill by his house. Still, this two-lane road was considered a state "highway." All he heard was an occasional bird chirping or squirrel rustling in the leaves. Chip had told him that the best time of year was fall, when all the leaves would turn red and yellow. It was pretty enough green.

After passing a canopy of trees arching over the main road like a tunnel of green, he finally saw the "town." But, just as his friend had said, Plymouth Hill was just a few buildings with wood shingle roofs along the road.

Alec headed to the largest building, across from the gas station. Over a red wood-paneled wall read "Corner Store."

As he opened the screen door, the bell jingled. At the sales counter, a middle-aged woman with long, curly red hair, wearing a very long, baggy dress, thumbed through her cellphone. She had a distinctive black half-circle symbol on her forehead.

"Morning," the woman said. "Vacationing? There's a small supply shop for boats and oars down the street—for the lake. Just ask Knoll at the gas station if you're here to go rowing or fishing. You can rent boats and oars from him. He even has fishing rods if you're an angler."

"I'm not vacationing. I'm staying."

Alec browsed a food aisle. There were various chips, candy, and gum. Not a whole lot of stuff other than snacks. He should have stocked up more food before his move.

At the far back of the store was a weird, eclectic section. This area was the most unique, reminding him of a magic shop. Here a large dark blue cloth with stars and moons was draped on the wall. And on two tables against the wall were various crystals, candles, and books.

"Stranger turning native?" the cashier asked. "You kiddin' me? I don't believe it. You know, there's only like ten of us in this whole damned town." She laughed. "Where you from?"

"L.A."

"L.A.? You went two thousand miles to live in the middle of nowhere?"

Alec returned to the food aisle and snatched a bag of salami, checking the expiration date. He shrugged.

"You're really moving here?"

"Yep. Up the hill."

"You're shacking up on Plymouth Crest!" she asked, laughing more than ever. He couldn't help but laugh too. "You're joking, right? That place has been vacant all my life."

"It's a great house."

"I thought maybe you were moving to Badger. You're really living up on Plymouth Crest? I don't believe it."

Alec nodded. He picked up a bag of plastic plates. It was then he realized there weren't any baskets, so he stacked the salami and a bag of chips on paper plates and laid it on the main counter

"Your store's close enough," he said with a grin.

But her mouth still gaped open, staring at him. That made him laugh again.

"My house is called Plymouth Crest?" he asked.

"The hill is called Plymouth Crest. Your house is called an abomination. It doesn't fit. Kind of like you." She raised a hand. "No offense. I just mean it's misplaced, you know. The house is as if some owner built a home in a city and plopped it down on our hill. People like climbing to the top just to dare themselves to go inside. They're afraid, 'cause it's said to be haunted, but they dare themselves to venture in anyway. I've been inside a few times. The house is beautiful, of course, but all the stuff inside looks spooky— chairs, tables—they're all ratty and decayed. Last time I was there, the lights turned on fine. Me and my friends were so impressed, being the place is so old. But watch out. People, especially kids from out of town, love to camp around there just to dare themselves to go in. Just to dare, you know. So don't freak out if drifters end up on your doorstep."

"That's creepy. You've been inside?"

"Sure…" She suddenly looked guilty. "Years ago. When the doors aren't locked. Everyone in town has been inside Plymouth Crest. It's open to visitors more often than you'd think. But you seem normal enough. A tall, dark, and handsome man from Hollywood, huh?" She smirked. "Short dark hair, blue eyes. You're cute."

"Thanks," Alec said, feeling taken aback. "But I'm not from Hollywood. I lived in the valley."

"Same thing. Can I help you get settled in? Most supplies around here are from Badger, but I've got a lot more here than it looks like. And I can order things too. It's about time someone decided to live up on that hill. No one's lived there for years."

"I just need food. I thought there'd be a market here."

"*A market in Plymouth Hill!?*" she said, slapping the counter with her palm, laughing harder than ever. "*A market?* You're funny, mister. Well, meet Plymouth Hill's market. Me. There's a Walmart in Badger. But I get plenty of business from drifters thinking the same thing you just did. And the main road here brings plenty of strangers. I thought you were just driving by like them. So…what do you do for a living, if you don't mind me asking? And what's your name?"

"I'm a writer," he said, grabbing a box of toothpicks by the front counter. "Name's Alec."

"A writer? But writers do other stuff, don't they?"

"I used to work as an accountant. I wrote on the side and then retired. Came here for peace and quiet."

That sent her barreling into laughter all over again.

"What's so funny?" he asked, chuckling too.

"Quiet? We sure have quiet. Sure have that: no people,

but loads of quiet. You know, there's just a handful of homes across the street. I live here. Well, I suppose we're neighbors now. Wow. Pleasure to meet you, Alec. Far out. And you're living up on Plymouth Crest? I don't believe it. If you need anything, anything, just holler. We all help each other in this boring town, especially 'round winter."

"I heard winters can get rough."

"They sure can. The elevation is high up here in the mountains. You can get snowed in with more than ten feet of snow for a week or two during a rough storm. Ever see *The Shining*? A few people go nutso like that. That's probably what keeps your place vacant. At least I'm by the road, so I talk to people vacationing around here all the time. A while ago, I knew a gentleman who lived at that house for only a few months. He left the place once the snow arrived. I've always guessed he got cabin fever. But don't worry. Cabin fever is all in the mind. No need to worry if you're sane. But also pretty cold winds can whip up, particularly around your house. Well, welcome, Alec. Welcome. Welcome to our quaint town of Plymouth Hill. You've come to the right place, I guess, if you were looking for nothing to do."

She put everything in a paper bag and handed it to him.

"Thanks."

"Hey, you want me to help you bring the stuff up to your house?" she asked, raising her brow. "I haven't been up to Plymouth Crest in so long. We can send it by 'Daisie's delivery service.'"

"What's 'Daisie's delivery service'?"

"That's my name. I'm Daisie."

"That's okay," Alec said with a laugh. "What's that symbol on your forehead?"

"It's a half-moon. Do you like it?"

He shrugged.

"I'm a witch. Don't worry, I'm a good witch. I'd be more worried about ghosts. And our winters. And cabin fever. But it didn't stop you from buying the place, did it? A woman died up there almost two decades ago, you know. She was from Hollywood too. Her name was—" Daisie put a finger to her chin and looked up for a moment. Then she shook her head. "Can't remember. She was some singer star turned actress that even made a few movies before moving here. Maybe trying to retire in peace and quiet? She and her lover probably went looney. Well, it's an old story I heard about when my parents moved here when I was, like, twelve. Me and my friends went up there quite often when I went to school in Badger. We wanted to see the ghost. Not much to do around Badger otherwise, as you can imagine. The haunting didn't stop you from buying the place?"

"Nope."

"I really love that, Alec. I really do. You're gutsy. You'd make a good warlock. Maybe I'll show you some magic one day. We can meet up in that house and do some rituals." And she winked.

"I don't believe in witches," he said with a chuckle.

"Yeah? But you believe in ghosts?"

THE APPLE THIEF

With the sun's rays shining between the green leaves of the trees surrounding the windows of his glass house, Plymouth Crest was enchanting. Gilded light shone through the leaves and branches creating yellow prism-like effects. And with all the green moss and thrush, it was enchanting—as if Alec lived in an English fae forest or Camelot, which he loved as a writer.

That was what happened during the day. But upon nightfall, all those large windows turned black. And then those same leaves and branches that covered the sunrays blocked moonlight. Then his house became very dark.

But not so quiet…

By the second week, he started hearing noises. At first, it was just stray creaks and cracks from the wood, and Alec figured it was simply the sound of an old foundation. But as time passed, he heard unexplainable things. Stray shouts and screams that sounded as if they were coming from the terrace outside. Doors opening and slamming shut downstairs. Kitchen cabinets left open. Plates and glasses being rearranged on the kitchen table. Doors left open all night. One morning, he even found the couch in the living room had been moved a couple feet. That was the creepiest. On yet another night, he awoke shivering. The glass balcony door of his bedroom was wide open. He was certain he had locked it.

As days passed, the noises only grew louder. One night a wooden chair tipped over downstairs in the dining room. Then another night, a plant was thrown from one of his tall cabinets in the foyer into the living room.

He began to not sleep. He didn't believe in ghosts, but he couldn't deny the noises.

Tonight, for hours, he had just stared at the white ceiling over his bed in silence. He had stared long enough for his eyes to adjust to the darkness. And after a while, the darkness made the faint moonlight that shone through openings in his dark mahogany velvet curtains seem bright.

His body jumped. His muscles reacted mechanically before he recognized the noise. It was glass shattering. Something had broken into pieces downstairs. It was so loud that he leapt out of bed and his hands scrambled along the walls to switch on the light. But the light wouldn't switch on. That was weird because his old clock on the nightstand still read one-thirty-two in red digital letters, and the clock didn't have back-up power. Electricity was another quirky thing about his house.

He opened the drawer in his nightstand by the bed. In his old house, he had always left a small flashlight by the bed. But the flashlight wasn't there. It was probably still in one of the boxes in the garage. And he had left his cellphone downstairs.

There was more opening and closing of cabinets and drawers. This time, it wasn't just stray noises, it seemed to be every few seconds. This didn't sound like the usual cracks and creaks of some phantom haunting his place. He was worried there was an actual intruder.

He rushed along the inner balcony. Most of his downstairs could be seen from here, but his furniture—his couch, end table, and chairs—were cast in shadows by moonlight.

"Who's down there?" Alec cried. "Show yourself."

He was answered by another crash. That made him move faster, darting across his dark, empty living room and running straight to the source of the noise—in the kitchen.

He was wearing only underwear and felt a breeze before seeing the open kitchen door. After doors being left open frequently over the past week, he was sure he had checked the lock on this door before going to bed. He rushed over to shut it.

"Sorry, I didn't realize anyone was home."

Alec whirled around. That made the intruder on the other side of the kitchen island cover her mouth and snicker.

He rushed over to turn on the kitchen light switch, but, oddly, it did not just turn on the kitchen lights, it switched on the digital display on the oven and the toaster and re-started a hum from the refrigerator. It's as if the light switch restarted the power in the whole house. And under the bright kitchen lights, Alec could now clearly discern a young lady, in her mid-twenties, leaning against the island. She had long dark hair and almond-shaped eyes. Her face was strikingly pretty. Beside her bare feet was a shattered glass cup—the glass that she must have broken. Being shoe-less under her navy blue snow coat with a fur-lined collar was strange. And she held a red apple in her hand—which she had stolen from his grocery bag, no doubt. Her mouth was curled in an amused smirk.

They stared at one another. Then she drew the apple up to her nose.

"What are you doing here?" Alec snapped.

"Eating an apple."

"No, what are you doing in my house?"

"Door was open," she said with a shrug. "Sorry about

the glass." And then she chuckled again, looking down at the shattered glass by her toes. "Have to be careful where I step now, I guess."

"Miss, this is private property."

She furrowed her brow and stared again, seeming to study him. Then her lips curled into that same amused smile. He wasn't sure what was so funny.

"Do I need to call the police?"

"Sheriff Denson?" she asked, bursting into laughter. "Are you fricken' kiddin' me? Denson can barely keep his pants on without suspenders. Speaking of pants."

She pointed an index finger at his body. It was then he remembered he was only wearing underwear. That made him angrier.

"I live here, miss! You're trespassing in my house."

"Aha," she said and turned her back on him. But she cocked her head back to catch a glimpse of his body.

"Gee-whiz," she said, sniffing her apple again, "I mean, I didn't think anybody stopped by this place anymore. I never had to worry about strangers before. I'm here all the time." She shrugged her shoulders. "You know, I roam—"

"In the middle of the night!"

"Hey, watch your tone, mister. I think you need to calm the hell down."

"Calm down? You're breaking into my house!"

"I'm not breaking into your house. There's never anyone here, I tell you. And the door was open. Okay already?"

She carefully stepped around the shards of broken glass. Then she roamed about the kitchen, picking up a decorative tray on the island and then a fake flower assortment. Examining everything. It was like she was inspecting the room. Then she opened a drawer and picked up a silver fork and knife. She opened a cabinet over one of the stoves and thumbed through more glasses.

"I sure like what you've done with the place," she said. "Not much different than what I would have done, I'd bet. You have really good taste."

"You scared the hell out of me."

"Man, I said sorry. You scared me too. Okay?"

She turned and faced him. They locked eyes again, and with her smirk, Alec had the sense that she was going to laugh in his face again.

"This is my house. You have to leave. Get the hell out or I'm calling the cops."

"Wow, you sure can be rude," she said, raising her hand. "Fine. Like I said, I didn't—"

Alec rushed her, hopping over the crushed glass and chasing her around the island. When she reached the glass again, she slowed and carefully hopped over it. He went to snatch her by the arm, but she burst into laughter as if they were playing chase and took off again, running another circle around the island before being chased out the door.

The game ended after Alec slammed the glass door on her face.

She scowled. Then she lifted her red apple over her head and intentionally dropped it on his mat outside. He answered by locking the door and fastening a chain lock.

When she oddly kept standing there, staring at him, he shouted, *"Go away!"*

The lights in the house switched off again.

Alec lay on his back in bed staring at the ceiling in the dark again. Now how could he get rest? Funny thing was, the creaking of the house had stopped. Still, every slide of a branch against the walls, or rustle of leaves by his bedroom window, made him stir.

The lady hadn't felt threatening, but her actions were. She had strutted around as if she owned the place.

He turned and gazed at the nightstand. His clock read four-twelve in the morning. The clock made him even more uneasy. The electricity was still out in the house. All the power wasn't working, except his clock. How? His digital clock had no backup power.

His cellphone buzzed on his nightstand. He rolled over to the side of the bed and picked up his phone. There were a few texts. One from his daughter, Rachel. It'd be around one o'clock in the morning in California. That one just read "call when u can." Another text was from Chip. But a third text, the most recent, was from an unknown caller. He figured the unknown caller was spam.

As he went to delete the message, he read in all caps, "*GO AWAY!*"

All the lights in his room switched on.

A FLASHLIGHT

IT WAS DRIZZLING. SOMETHING NOT TOO UNFAMILIAR IN Plymouth Hill, according to Daisie, but it dampened Alec's plans to hike down to her Corner Store in the morning. So he drove his gray Lexus SUV down the winding road to her store. After he parked in the muddy dirt lot, he opened the screen door. And, as always, she stood behind her sales counter, now reading a small black book with stars on the cover.

Daisie was becoming a good friend. There weren't many people to talk to in town, but there was always Daisie. And Daisie was a lot of fun. On some days, he spent hours at a time just talking to her about weather, politics, movies, and all sorts of random stuff. Not just because the woman was easy to converse with, but because she was the only person to talk to.

"Raining in July, huh?" asked Alec, shaking his head.

"Raining in July." Daisie put down her book. She heaved a sigh. "Raining in August. Raining in September. Raining in October. Raining in November. I told you about rain here. Wait till it snows, Alec. Then it'll be snowing in December, January, February, March, April, and maybe

May. If you're lucky, you'll get clear skies in June. When does it ever not fucking rain or snow in Plymouth Hill?"

He chuckled.

"It's good to see you," she said with a smile. "Life alone on the top of your hill giving you cabin fever yet?"

"No, I love it."

"Hmm. How do you spend all your boring time? Oh yeah, writing."

"Well, not getting as much writing done as I dreamed. But trying."

Daisie walked around the counter and over to his aisle. She was wearing another draping dress. This one was lime green. It was striking with her red hair. And, as usual, she had a moon drawn on her forehead.

"What'cha looking for?" she asked with hands on hips. "I'll give you Daisie's special service."

"A flashlight."

"Whatcha need a flashlight for?"

"The power keeps going out at the house."

"Huh…hey, I've got an amazing one in the back. Hold on. I got one that can light up an entire baseball field. You want that one? You could probably go hunting with it. Do you hunt? People from the city come here to hunt all the time. Aside from fishing on the lake, that's what our boring town's all about. I'd rather sell you a flashlight in the back than one of these stupid small plastic thingies, Alec. But doesn't your cellphone have a flashlight?"

"I just need a simple light at night."

"Why not just use your cellphone?"

"I don't like carrying my phone around everywhere."

"Oh yeah. Your house is huge." But she slowly nodded, looking at him as if he were crazy. With the moon drawn on her head. He laughed. "I suggest you change your habits and just carry your cellphone in a pocket everywhere you go, Alec."

"You're not trying hard to sell me stuff."

"Well, I don't often sell flashlights," she said with a shrug. "Who the hell buys a flashlight these days? That's like buying cameras. Unless you get one of them special ones, like I've got in the back."

"The lights keep going out." That made him shudder. Because it reminded him of the intruder. "That reminds me. I wanted to ask you something. One of those bohemians you were talking about came by the house in the middle of the night a few days ago. She was so brazen that she walked right into my kitchen, stole one of my apples, and started eating it in front of my face. I couldn't believe it. I almost called the police, but I was able to just chase her out."

"I told you drifters are all over Plymouth Hill. That won't be the last. But Sheriff Denson wouldn't have done anything. Did you catch the apple thief's name? Maybe she's local and I'd recognize her name."

"No," he said with a chuckle. "I was too busy throwing her out. But she must live around here. She mentioned the sheriff's name."

"Like I said, lots of weird people live around Badger. Look at me."

"I threw her out. But..." He debated whether to tell her.

"But what?"

"She texted me. Or I think she texted me. It really was disturbing... I got a message after she left, on my phone, saying, '*Go away*.' My phone read an unlisted number, but the text came to me right after seeing her."

"Why would the words '*go away*' freak you out? If she was some stalker, it would have said something like '*I'm coming after you*.'"

"Because I shouted those exact words at her when I

locked the door on her. It was all too weird to be a coincidence. But how did she get my phone number?"

Daisie grimaced.

"Honestly, Alec, I can't believe you're still up there on that hill. I would have wagered you'd be flying back home in a month. I told you, people go bonkers up here. Wait till winter. Maybe you saw your ghost? Just...just you wait a minute. Let me show you the amazing flashlight I've got stored in the back. You've gotta see it. It's such a beauty. I won't feel bad selling it to you, not as much as one of those small plastic thingies. I tell you, this thing can light up your whole hilltop. Just don't shine it directly into your eyeballs. It probably could blind you too." She laughed. "Hey, come to think of it, you could use it as a weapon to blind the next apple thief."

"Okay, sure," he said with a chuckle.

"Be back in a jiffy," she said with a wink. Then she walked around the counter and passed through a wooden door at the back of her store.

"You don't think it's weird that an unlisted number texted me the last words I said to the stranger?" he hollered.

He heard her in the other room rummaging through boxes.

"There's nothing special about the words *go away*," she said from the other room. "It's probably a coincidence."

"Just the whole thing was so strange. She acted like... eating that apple in my kitchen, she was acting like, I don't know, as if it was her house."

"I told you people are strange around here. Or maybe you saw your ghost, Alec. Yeah, maybe it was the ghost. Just because you don't believe in ghosts doesn't mean they don't exist." She laughed, still rummaging through things in the adjacent room. "You live in a haunted house.

Remember? Yeah, maybe it wasn't a drifter? Maybe it was the ghost. A ghost that likes apples."

"You really think she was the ghost? I thought about that, but I can't believe it. She was too real, Daisie. I tell you, she was flesh and blood, right in front of me, just like you are."

"No, she was probably one of those drifters camping out around your house. Your house is not only a beauty, it's at the top of the woods with a magnificent view. Keep all your windows and doors locked. Maybe get a watchdog. Or install some cameras—hey, I might be able to get you some of those for real cheap too. I got an Alec-Daisie sale going on all week." She chuckled. "And then just... *fuck!* Give me one second. Where the hell did I leave that box? Tells you how strange it is to ask for flashlights. Geeze, I really like you, Alec. You're so weird. I like that a lot. You're not a usual guy, you know. Like I'm not your usual gal... goddamn it, where did I leave that thing? I tell you, this flashlight can burn a hole in your intruder's eyeball. It's like a light saber."

"Okay," he said with another chuckle.

"Nope," she muttered, walking back into the store. "Alec, sorry, it's not back with my supplies."

Then she stood behind the counter and dug her fingers through her long red hair. When she raised her head, she looked into his eyes and grinned.

"Hey, are you going to Badger for the fireworks show next weekend?"

"I didn't know about it."

"It's our Fourth of July fireworks show, Alec. It's a real special get-together for everybody around here. You want to go with me?"

IT'S REALLY NOT YOURS

A LEC SAT ON HIS LEATHER COUCH, GAZING OUT HIS LIVING room window at the forest in his backyard. It was early in the morning, and a thin mist fogged the surrounding trees and thick green foliage along the grounds. Morning fog was something else he was starting to get accustomed to on Plymouth Crest, another beautiful thing about the house. If he had been able to see the lake, he might have seen what looked like wisps of smoke skating along the surface of the water. It was all breathtaking. But that made him feel worse. Because it was a view that, apparently, he couldn't have.

"You can't close escrow?" Alec snapped, leaning his head in his hands and rubbing his eyes. "I can't believe this."

Chip and his guest looked miserable too, sitting across from the sofa in matching black leather lounge chairs. His best friend wore a formal navy blue suit with his dark hair perfectly combed. The young kid, probably not much older than twenty, had a shaved head, tattoos running along his neck and right cheek, and a distinctive ring in his right eyebrow. He looked young enough to be Chip's son.

"You told me everything was done, Chip," Alec said, running his hand through his thin hair. "I never would have moved all my stuff in had I known about this."

"Calm down, man," Chip said, raising his hand. "We can still close. It's just a formality."

"Dad never signed the property over to me, that's all," said the kid with a chuckle. "But the law should give me the property, right?"

"You're asking me?" Alec asked, leaning forward. "You're the one who put the house up for sale."

"You don't have ownership, Robin," Chip said, shaking his head. "You told me you had full title and then you signed documents, but it means nothing if you don't hold the deed."

"But the house had to go to Dad after the owner's death. And I've been selling Dad's stuff for years. I sold all his furniture in the house without any problems."

"How can you enter escrow without looking into all this?" cried Alec to Chip in disbelief, hitting the coffee table. But then he glanced at the kid. "You never entered probate with your dad's estate?"

"Why would I do that?"

"*Who is the fucking owner of my house!*" Alec shouted, jumping up.

That was followed by a loud crash upstairs. It sounded as if the dresser in the bedroom had toppled over. Then the ceiling and walls rumbled. The explosion made Chip and Robin look up, but Alec fell back on the couch and put his head in his hands again. He was getting so used to these noises that it hardly fazed him.

"Wow," Robin said, looking up. "The house really is haunted."

"Should we check upstairs?" suggested Chip.

Alec shook his head, running his fingers through his short hair again.

"Look, Dad disappeared after leaving the country years ago," Robin said. "I assumed everything in his estate went to me, including the house. Who else would get it?"

"You said your dad disappeared," Alec replied, glancing up at him. "Do you have paperwork showing transfer of title to you? Or his will? I just need the sale in writing so you can transfer this house over to me."

Then Robin made Alec feel worse by staring stupidly at him.

"Chip?" Alec asked, rolling his eyes. "I paid loads of money for the movers to haul all my stuff from California. I even had the car delivered. Now you want me to pay the rest of the money I owe for the house when you can't close escrow? When you can't get the deed for the house. Have you lost your fucking mind?"

"You've been in the house for weeks," Robin said. "Seems it's your house to enjoy."

Alec ignored his guest. Instead, he stared at his friend, dumbfounded. Chip avoided his gaze, staring out the window at the lovely view of the woods. *Again*, the spectacular yard he was now being told he couldn't have.

"Look, you don't have to leave," Robin said. "Just stay put and enjoy the place. You just need to transfer the rest of my money. Leave all your stuff here. I don't mind. I just need final payment."

"You don't own the fucking place, you idiot!"

"Hey!" Robin cried, jumping up. "Really? You have no right talking to me like that."

"Oh, I'm sorry, am I getting you upset?"

"Look," Robin said. He looked over at Chip, but Chip was staring down at the carpet again. "Look, Dad went missing... I've sold lots of his stuff without any trouble."

"Get the paperwork," Alec said. "Or hire an attorney and prove ownership, otherwise I won't pay you a dime. And you'll owe me my deposit back."

"I think you're making a big deal over nothing," Robin said. "This is all just a formality."

"Alec's profession was based on formalities," said Chip with a shrug.

"Seriously?" Alec snapped. "You don't agree with me, Chip? You said everything was ready to go. I figured you'd hand over the deed to the house this morning. Now you return here telling me the owner might not be the owner."

"I flew back here from L.A. to tell you, Alec," he said, raising his brow. "Jesus, look, I'm not pleased about all this either."

"Why hasn't the state taken the house if the owner left the country?" Alec asked Chip. "Maybe it's because there's an owner who still owns it who's not this kid? Maybe we just need to find the owner?"

"Dad hasn't spoken to me—"

"I wouldn't either."

"Hey, fuck off, man!" Robin cried. "I don't need your shit. Yeah, I'll get a lawyer, all right, if you don't pay up. You moved in. You signed escrow. The deal was made when you gave me your deposit. Everything is ready to go."

"Get out!" Alec shouted. "Neither of us owns this place."

And that's just what Robin did. He rushed out of the living room, threw open the front door, and slammed it behind him.

"God, Chip," Alec said running his fingers through his hair, "man, did you even meet this guy in person before signing?"

But Chip sank down in the chair. Then he put his head in his hands just like Alec had.

"Everything was done by email," Chip said. "I told you, he forged some of the documents. I didn't know it till it didn't go through at the bank. I would never have gotten you into this, had I known. Robin wants to make the deal. I mean, he traveled all the way over here, in the middle of nowhere, to do that. He might still be able to get legal ownership, as he's the closest kin I've been able to find."

"*Fuck!*" Alec leaned back in the sofa. "Chip…just go figure things out! No wonder the kid was selling at such a low price. It's not only haunted, it's not his house to sell."

"Yeah," Chip said, getting up. He patted Alec on the back. "Sure. Look, I'm sorry, man."

"Just… Just find the owner."

There was another rumble upstairs.

"Is that the noises you were talking about? That's the stuff keeping you up at night?" asked Chip, looking up. "How do you sleep at all? Jesus, it doesn't even seem to faze you."

"I…I've gotten used to it. Look, I still love this place. Find the owner so we can sign off and be done with this. I still want the house."

"I already found the owner," Chip said. "But telling you about it is not going to make you feel any better."

"Who is it?"

"The house was built and owned by a pop star. Her name was Fifi. Fifi Graynger. Ever heard of her? You might have heard some of her music. But we were never into pop, we were more into alternative music back in college. Fifi was in Hollywood too. Remember, Alec, the B-movies she did? *Lowry and the Cat.* That was a musical comedy about a stowaway talking cat. That was her biggest hit. That film *Idling off Soho* was good too. She was a really funny girl. Not only with an amazing voice, but cute as hell. Of course her music career is where she really got her fame. Well, she disappeared twenty years ago. Locals claim she committed suicide in your house, but there's no death certificate. Believe me, I've looked. Legally, she's missing. Sort of. Well, if she's missing, someone's been forging her signatures and paying her taxes. That's how I got so far into the deal without becoming suspicious. The banks just assumed the mortgage was legit. No one's been checking out the late Fifi, probably because all the bills are getting paid off so—I mean look at this so-called town—who the hell's going to investigate? I have loads of paperwork in her name, but the mystery is only going to send us sliding into a bigger rabbit hole. There's no explanation for how Fifi has continued to keep up the place, how's she's paying, or where she's disappeared to—if she's alive. It's a really weird mystery. And it hardly helps our situation, buddy. We need to have the owner to buy the house. As you said, it doesn't matter who the hell that owner is as long as they can sell it to you."

"It's like the dust," Alec said pensively, walking slowly over to the window. He stared out at the woods again. "Someone's been taking care of this place."

"I suppose. It's strange Robin didn't know all about it. The kid genuinely thought he was the de facto owner, and that he could work stuff out with the bank, as he's the son of Fifi's lover."

"Look for her. Or whoever's claiming to be her. We can work out all the legal shit when we find out who's maintaining the place. Maybe if we find that, we can have the house sold to us. Or, if this music star's missing, perhaps you can find—"

"You want me to find a pop star who disappeared over twenty years ago? She had a lot of fans, Alec. Don't you think her fans looked for her? Yes, there's paperwork with her recent signatures, but there's also stories about the house. According to the locals and rumors, Fifi committed suicide here. She's the ghost I warned you about when you opened escrow."

"That doesn't explain the upkeep. Maybe she's one of those famous stars that wanted to feign her death to be free of the spotlight? Maybe she faked her death for privacy? Dig deeper, Chip."

"I will," Chip said, heaving a sigh. "Sure. I will."

"I'm sorry I yelled at you," Alec muttered. "I didn't mean to be a jerk, but I've really been growing fond of this place."

"Don't worry about me, my friend, worry about Robin. You really pissed him off good. If there's anything still tying him to ownership and our sale, I don't think he's coming back."

"Do you blame me?"

"Nope. No, I don't." Chip took a deep breath, jumped up, and walked to the window. He shook his head, staring at the yard. "I'll make things right, man. You'll still get this house. Don't worry."

"Yeah, well… I'm sorry about yelling at the kid too." He jumped up and walked to the window to stare at the gorgeous view. "I was just so upset. I want this house. But I really didn't mean to shout at him. That was wrong."

"It's your anger problem."

"Sure," he said solemnly, nodding and still staring at the view.

"Don't be so worried, man. We'll figure all this out, still get you the house and close escrow."

"You asked me not to worry last time."

"Well, this time I mean it. We have leads, I just need to dig deeper. And, anyway, without anyone claiming the place, you don't have to move."

THE LADY BY THE LAKE

Alec sat on large rocks hanging over the shore of the lake with his computer on his lap. It was a lovely rocky outlook reaching about ten yards over the water, like a little natural pier. He had tried to write yesterday on a plastic chair on his balcony, with the same amazing view, but failed miserably. He thought perhaps sitting right at the lake would awaken his muse. Nope. Too beautiful. Birds chirped, leaves rustled, and it was quiet enough to hear the gentle lapping of the water. It smelled woodsy with an almost vanilla scent. He remembered that wonderful fresh air smell from when he used to visit the woods in the mountains in California. Rachel had reminded him about that in their conversation the other day, when he was trying to describe the forest smell to her. He already loved Plymouth Crest so much. But that only made him angrier when he thought about how he might have to leave.

A small bird hopped over some rocks and splashed near the water. Then he felt a cool, gentle breeze brush over his hair and beard on the right side of his face. He turned. For some reason, he felt like he was being watched. All he saw were the branches of nearby trees gently swaying.

As far as writing, things weren't going so well. He'd thought he was going to get so much writing done away from the noise in the city. He stared at the blank screen on his laptop.

"Beautiful, isn't it?"

Alec jumped. Then he nearly fell into the water. Looking to his right again, only ten feet away, stood a lady in a long thin white dress flowing down to her bare feet. She was hardly paying any attention to him. She was just squinting and staring at the glistening lake. The yellow light reflected, almost glowed, over her smiling face. It was her! It was the intruder who had broken into his house.

"Are you following me?" Alec snapped.

"I live here," she said, cocking her head back. Then she wrapped her arms around herself, closed her eyes, and smiled wider. "Smells so nice. It's so beautiful in the morning, isn't it? Near midday now, I suppose. I love mornings here by the lake. And summer is so nice and bright around Plymouth Crest, isn't it?" She looked back at him and nodded. "I would have explained myself further, had you not thrown the door in my face. That was very rude."

Alec said nothing. He just stared.

"I love this lake so much," she added. "Don't you?"

"Yes."

She giggled and nodded again, turning back to the view. Then she just stared out over the lake, ignoring him again.

Had this been some other stranger, particularly after breaking into his home, he would have raged at her or shoved her into the water. Not her. With her thin white dress reflecting the yellow rays of the sun, she was radiant, glimmering like a shining white-robed goddess. Wind brushed gently over her long dark hair. Her sleeves flowed down her arms to lace cuffs, seeming light, bright, and almost translucent as if they barely covered her arms. She was not only pretty, she seemed dazzling, like the lake. No, more like she *was* the lake. Under the bright rays of the sun, he could now better discern her face. Her skin was tanned, contrasting with her white clothes. She had narrow features, with a thin nose and dark eyebrows over almond eyes. Her eyes seemed sharp, marked with intelligence. And now those blue eyes just stared over the water. He felt that if he got up and headed back to the house, she wouldn't move. She would still be standing there, like a tree or stone, as if she were a fixture over the water. Her lips were her most striking feature, bright red, but seemingly always curved in a whimsical grin, as if curling over some joke that seemed to always be on him. But, whatever was so funny, even if she was poking fun at him, he liked her whimsical mood. She seemed so full of energy.

He found himself as mesmerized by staring at her as by Plymouth Crest itself. And it didn't really matter that she had broken into his home the other night. He didn't want her to leave. He'd be happy if she just stood with him, gazing out from the shore, the rest of the day.

"What?" She cocked her head and threw her long dark hair back.

"Who are you?"

"It wasn't right for that house to be sold to you," she said, brushing hair from her eyes and looking stern. "Particularly by a clod. That boy had no right to sell it, to tell you the truth. It's not his. Not even his dad's. Nothing idiots with fancy suits and signatures are gonna fabricate will change that. It belongs to whom it's always belonged to."

"My name's Alec," he drawled. "Let me try again. Who…what is your name? And, where—"

"Joy," she said with a nod. Then she furrowed her brow. "What are you typing on that computer?"

"Are you following me?"

"No one owns anything here. The house is like the lake.

None of it really belongs to anyone." And she nodded then hugged herself again, gazing over the water. "That's why it's so absolutely wonderful. The house *is*. The lake *is*. Everything just *is*. It always is and always shall be. There's something so wonderful about that, isn't there? Permanence. It has nothing to do with ownership or anything human really. It just is. And I love that. If people would stop what they're doing and enjoy the moment, stop trying to think or own things, what trouble would they ever have?"

"What are you talking about? What's your name?"

"I told you my name. I'm Joy."

"Joy, how did you know there was something up with my purchasing agreement for my house? And what business is it of yours?"

"I read it. It was—"Then she spoke in a British accent —"*bollocks*, as the Brits say. The house is not owned by that kid or his dad."

"You read my purchase agreement? How? By breaking into my house again?"

"Stop," she said, raising a hand. "You're really on edge a lot, aren't you? That's one thing I don't like about you, Alec. You have a bit of a temper and can turn mean."

"How did you read it?" he asked, feeling angrier. "Was this after you broke into my house? Or did you break into my house again?"

"You mean when *you* came to the house, stranger. No one lived there for years. I told you already, a million times, that no one alive owns that house. It's like this lake. It just is. And that's how it will stay. Isn't that beautiful?"

"Where do you live, miss? Who are you? Stop fooling around. I was told there aren't any homes for miles. Plymouth Hill has a couple homes, but that's two miles from here. How come you keep acting like you live at my house?"

"Maybe I should question you. Why did you travel all the way across the country to sit before a lake and write? Do you think that's all that life's about? Writing by yourself over a lake? Staring at your reflection in the water. Seems a bit selfish, don't you think? What about your daughter back home, with her baby coming? Why not go back home to California and be there for her? That reminds me of my family."

"*How do you know about my daughter?*"

"Oops." She put her hand over her mouth. Then she snickered. "Well…well, I mean, you were talking to her on the phone."

"*When?*"

She shrugged. "Well—I mean…"

"Did you break into my house again? Are you spying on me?"

"Won't you calm the hell down?"

"The house is mine, miss," he said. "You can't be trespassing—"

"Calm down," she said, raising a hand. "Geesh. Fine. Whatever. You win. I suppose you got a problem seeing a woman here by your lake too? Am I not allowed here either? Do you own the lake? As if the lake isn't big enough for the two of us. You know, I was beginning to like you, Alec, but you need to be friendlier in a small town like Plymouth Hill. Anyway—" She turned from him and frowned. "Seems we're getting off on the wrong foot. Welcome to Plymouth Hill."

He just stared at her. Then he slammed shut his laptop, tucked it under his arm, got up, and made his way back up the trail to his home.

"You're creepy."

"You go have a nice life too."

He made his way back to the trail that led to the main road and then up the hill to his house.

"You can be a real asshole, Alec."

That made him look back. She shook her head, appearing stern, and quipped, "Good luck with your book."

Then she turned around, faced the lake, and held herself in her arms again. He gazed back at her when he was higher up the hillside, and she looked like she had when he first saw the house. She seemed to just be happy enjoying the view alone, as if she had never spoken to him.

DATE'S OUT COLD

Alec. He really didn't seem to care. It seemed the question was simply to strike up conversation.

Sheriff Denson had a look of suspicion on his face—that same look of distrust Alec had seen in the rest of the bunch tonight. Denson was an older gray-haired man wearing suspenders. For Plymouth Hill, he *was* the police. Yep, the sheriff of Badger was here, along with nearly all the others from the town, at their local Fourth of July party. Many sat on logs, others were cross-legged on the grass, but everyone circled around three large bonfires.

They were on an overlook far up in the mountains, at a much higher elevation than his house. It was a small glade, the ground mostly dirt and leaves. They had all hiked ten minutes up a trail after trudging through the deep forest. A young guy named Jed had told everyone he was a hunter. They had all followed him. Jason, his brother, even wore a hunter's hat.

Silvia and Garth seemed to be the nicest couple of the group, striking up conversation with everybody. They were a young dark-skinned couple with Latino accents. They had moved from Tampa to Badger just five years ago. They were vaping weed by the bonfire with Sheriff Denson.

Frazier was the most boisterous of the pack, engaging everybody with music, cards, footballs, frisbees, or whatever he could think of to maintain fun. He was a tall, very dark-skinned man in a brown wool sweater. And he was the organizer of the whole debacle. The city doctor was there too. Doctor Norman. Everyone called him Normie. And another couple, sitting near Alec and the sheriff, facing the valley, was Ted and Francis. That couple sat beside another couple, Donna and Terry. Both couples were hay farmers living in Badger. There were many, many others. He couldn't recall all their names. But everyone knew each other as if they were family.

Far down the hillside were rooftops camouflaged by the green forest canopy and a few streetlights under the starry night. These structures made up the town of Badger.

Alec gazed up at the night sky and took a deep breath, taking in the fresh air. One of the greatest things about living in a rural area, ever since moving to Plymouth Crest, was the star-filled sky. He'd sometimes sit on his balcony, just gazing up at all those stars, late into the night.

Alec had mistakenly thought Daisie had invited him to an organized firework show. That presumption had ended after Frazier presented a duffel bag full of firecrackers.

"Yeah, I'm a writer," Alec finally answered the sheriff. He hadn't replied for so long that it seemed to take the sheriff a second to remember what he had asked. "It's so nice out here at night."

"What do you write?"

"I started with mystery short stories for magazines. And an article here and there in some writing journals. Then I tried science fiction novels for a while with some A.I. stuff. Now I delve more into romance."

"He's very good," Daisie said with a slightly slurred

voice, sitting beside him. She ran her fingers over his shoulder.

"How would you know?" Alec asked Daisie, amused.

"Just do," she answered with a wink. "Just do." Daisie swayed, seeming to have difficulty staying seated. "I just know." Then she patted his back.

Daisie had a flamboyant dress, this one rainbow colored, and was wearing a little too much dark makeup—and, of course, she had that distinctive moon drawn on her forehead.

"When are you going to invite us to your place?" asked Jed. "I haven't been in your house up there on Plymouth Crest for a long time."

"Seems everyone's been inside my house," Alec said with a laugh. "Daisie told me people have been breaking and entering for decades. You guys can come up whenever you want."

"That's why I'm sure glad you're finally living there," said Sheriff Denson, raising his beer can as if in a toast. "Now that someone's living at the place, I don't have to keep coming every time some idiot thinks they saw a ghost. You don't know how often people are making trouble reporting sightings. Many go there just to try to see the spirits."

"There are ghosts there," said Dr. Norman. "I saw a shadow through the windows when traveling around the summit of Plymouth Crest a couple years ago. I swear, it was just standing and glowing behind the window staring up at me. The place is damned creepy, if you ask me. Damned creepy." He smirked at Alec. "Good luck to you, sir."

"Remember when we broke into the house for our New Year's party a few years back, Sheriff?" Jason asked.

"That was fun," Denson replied with a nod.

Now Alec understood why the whole town disparaged

Sheriff Denson. He seemed to talk about nothing but breaking the law.

"Alec?" Daisie whispered in his ear. "Alec? Alec, I really need to go to the lady's room. Can you come with me?"

He turned to her and furrowed his brow. Daisie looked pale.

"I need to go, like, *now*," she said quietly. "I don't feel good."

Alec nodded, got up, and took her by the hand.

"We'll be right back," Alec said to the group.

"Not till you tell us when we're invited up to your house," said Jed with a laugh. But Jed raised his beer can as if in a toast.

"You're welcome anytime," Alec said with a laugh, walking with Daisie deeper into the woods.

That was followed by another explosion. Someone shouted and everyone scattered looking up in terror. A rocket was flying straight up over the group. Thankfully, the firecracker fell off the cliffside. Everyone laughed. Then they started yelling at Frazier.

Daisie held Alec close in her arms as they wandered among the trees and through the thicket. She kept stumbling, tripping over branches and bushes.

"*Tha-nks Alec*," she drawled, squinting up at his face. Then she reached up and touched his cheek, stroking his beard. "You're so nice. I think I drank just a little bit too much tonight."

When they were deep enough into the woods that it was difficult to make out the group, she surprised him by pushing him up against a tree trunk. There, she started clambering all over his body, kissing his neck and lips like crazy.

"Stop it, Daisie!" he snapped, pushing her off him. "Stop!"

"Sorry," she said with a burp. "Sorry... Alec." Then

she put her hand on her forehead. "Sorry, I just, you know, can't help myself around a handsome man like you. We're still friends, though, right?"

"Are you okay?"

"No," she said with a chuckle. "No, I'm really not, Alec."

Then she opened her eyes wide, pushed herself away from his chest, and rushed to a bush under a thick tree trunk. She threw up.

Alec stood over her. To his right, he could still hear the laughter and barely make out the campfire about thirty yards through dense foliage.

"Sorry," Daisie said, leaning over, retching some more. "You're so damn nice. I'm really sorry I…kissed you. I just. I just drank…so frickin' fuckin' much, I think. But you are cute, you see. But we're just friends. I know."

"We are friends, Daisie. And I think I need to take you home."

"You can't do that," she said, holding his hand. "You've been…hey, you've been drinking too. I'll just suffer a little bit more. You go back with the others, and I'll just sit here by my lonesome. Nothing's happening here."

"I'm not leaving you. Maybe we can get Frazier to drive you now rather than later?"

"Are you kiddin' me? He's here to entertain. Ain't he funny?"

"What about the doctor?"

"*Normie? Normie!*" she cried, laughing like crazy. "He's fuckin' drinking too, Alec! Do you like 'em all? Huh? Do you like my friends? Everyone's nice but they…get tiresome. You know, they're totally like family. Shit, I've been here the longest in this dull, rotten town…I think. Just this fuckin' town wears you down after a while. I always tell you that, but you stick around for some reason. Let me tell you a secret." And she cupped her hands around her lips. Then she didn't say anything at all. She just furrowed her brow. She looked around, covered her mouth, and burped. Finally she said, "I love… I love, love, love, love, I just love it that you love being here. Nothing's really new, 'xcept you. And…but you'll learn every holiday's the same. Over and over. Guess what we all do for Thanksgiving? Guess. Go ahead, Alec. Take a guess. It'll be familiar. What do you think we do at every holiday?"

He shrugged.

"*That's it! That's what we do!*" she said, laughing and slapping her knee. "Nothing. Absolutely nothing. We drink around a table, shooting the breeze, talking 'bout absolute nothing. It's funny cause many people leave their old families to come here and live alone, only to find that the town itself becomes their family. You'll find that out soon enough. You just have to be careful you don't piss anyone off." She laughed. Then she covered her mouth and burped. "You just—"

"Francis and Ted are nice."

"Ted? Ted? He fucking cheats on his wife, Alec. Come on. You know better. He's a sneaky little fucker. Whenever a new girl arrives in town, he's all over her." She looked dreamily up into his eyes. Then she wiped her mouth. "Sorry. You don't seem to like it when I cuss. You're such a sweet man. Anyway…things aren't always what they seem. You're just too damn nice to notice." She tried to get up, but she swooned. "Damn, I drank *waaaay* too much tonight."

"Everyone's nice."

"Thanks for staying with me. I feel safe around you. The forest has dangers for a gal, ya know. You can go back to the others. I'll just rest here…for a little…while."

And then she just lay on her side under a tree. She closed her eyes. In another moment, she started snoring.

There was another explosion. That was followed by another burst of laughter from the group by the cliffside.

"She's got a point," said another stranger's voice. "These woods aren't as safe as they sometimes seem."

There in the shadows, by two trees, was a lady. His lady by the lake! Joy! She stood only about ten feet away, leaning against a tree trunk with hands in her pockets, wearing a black blouse and jeans. But even in darkness, her eyes, contrasting with her long dark hair, seemed to glow aqua blue—those inquisitive, sharp bright eyes.

Although he had shouted at her by the shore, he wasn't upset to see her. The feeling in his chest was like what he had felt when Chip first showed him his house. It wasn't anger at all. He felt happy.

"Afraid your date's out cold," she said, pointing an index finger at Daisie with a chuckle. "And you've been drinking a bit too much yourself, Alec. Shame on you. Is your car around here? I can drive you both home."

"What..." Alec looked all around him. "How...where did you come from, Joy?"

"This town doesn't care for me much," she said bitterly. "Not like her. She's native. She's as much a fixture as Plymouth Crest is to folks around here. Daisie could never be an outsider, like you and me, Alec. That's the thing about Badger. You'll always be an outsider if you weren't born or raised here. You and I will always be crazy Californians to all of them."

"You're from California?"

"Sure," she said, coming closer and waving her hair from her eyes. "Sometimes," she said in a near-whisper, "I'll tell you a little secret. Sometimes, I come by just to watch everyone make fools of themselves, especially during the holidays when they get drunk." She laughed, looking down at Daisie. "They're funny, like her. There's a few others, like Knoll at the gas station, who don't socialize, more like me. Even his dullness and dreariness can be refreshing. Sometimes. But that's about it. Not much else about us, really. Just trees. And our lake. Now you know everybody and everything there is to know about our small town."

And Joy laughed again. Her laughter made him laugh too.

Then he felt himself tremble as she walked very close to him. She seemed to glow, drawing down the moonlight as she searched his eyes.

"Do you…still…hate me?"

"What?"

"*Do you…hate me?*" she drawled with a big grin.

"Why would I hate you?"

"Because I broke into your home? I tried to apologize again by the lake, but I just managed to upset you more. I'm sorry. All that stuff about the contracts, I just learned when you were on the phone earlier in the day, with your daughter, when I did my morning walk. You talk to her a lot. I walk by the house every morning, hearing you calling her. That's all. But I haven't broken in since. I promise. You know, I just like to wander around the grounds of your place."

Daisie groaned. They both looked down as Daisie closed her eyes tighter, stirring on the leaves. That made Joy chuckle again.

"Wow," Joy said, shaking her head. "She is so fucked up. Good for her. Like I've said ever since I was little, you should enjoy yourself in life."

Joy gazed back up into his eyes again. And they just stared into each other's eyes for a moment. The only thing to move was Joy's lips. Her lips seemed to curl even more into a grin.

"Why don't you let me drive you home?" she asked.

"What?"

"*Why don't you let me drive you home?*" she drawled again, lifting her brow. "I owe you for all the trouble I caused you."

They heard yet another firecracker, and the group through the trees roared with another burst of laughter.

Alec looked down at Daisie. She was still sound asleep.

"All right, Joy."

HUMMING

JOY DIDN'T SAY A WORD. THE WHOLE WAY DOWN THE CURVY road, hugging the woodland mountain, back through Badger, and then up his hill to Plymouth Crest, she didn't say one word. She just hummed.

Her voice was amazing. Alec sat in the back seat behind Daisie, watching as Joy held the wheel with both hands, carefully watching the road and humming. He didn't recognize the tune, but her voice was enchanting. It was tranquil and so soothing. Or…maybe he was deceived after drinking so much? His eyes kept fighting to stay open…

No. Whatever she was humming, it was so melodic and so beautiful. It put him at ease. He forced himself awake just to listen.

"What is that you're singing?" Alec asked in a hushed voice.

"Hmm?" Joy asked, cocking her head back.

"What is it that you're humming?"

"Oh, it's just some tune I made up in my brain. I make up lots of music in my mind. Sometimes whole songs. Sometimes even whole albums come into my head in the shower. I'm kinda weird that way. Do you like it, Alec?"

She cocked her head back again and smiled. Then she winked.

"Yeah, I do."

"I'll try not to forget how it goes then," she said with a nod. Then she raised a finger and mimed making a checkmark in the air, as if marking a list.

Alec laughed a bit too loud and covered his mouth. Daisie stirred in the passenger seat.

"What?" asked Daisie. "What's going on? Are we back—"

"We're driving you home," Alec said, leaning forward. "Don't worry."

Daisie just nodded and fell backward in the passenger seat.

Then Joy went back to quietly humming. It was that same wonderful tune that the young lady claimed she had made up. And Alec just sat back and loved watching and listening to her.

TROUBLED STEPS

ALEC PRACTICALLY DRAGGED DAISIE UP THE FRONT YARD along the concrete walkway to his house. Daisie was attempting to use her feet, sort of tripping along, but Alec kept shushing her, worried that she wouldn't watch where she was going if she didn't focus on the ground. Alec wasn't really all that steady either. All the while, Joy trailed behind, following him up the path to the front door. As the automatic lights lit up Alec's front porch, Alec fumbled with his keys by the front door.

"Hey," Daisie slurred, "hey, just you wait one second, misser. This isn't…this isn't my fuggin' house. Are you tryin' to take advantage of me, Alec?" She grimaced, looking up at him. "Ain't this your haunted house?"

Joy laughed behind them.

"We got a ride back and I figured I'd watch you for a little while," Alec said. "When you're better, I'll drive you home back down the hill."

"Aw, you're so nice."

He opened the door and Joy switched on the light behind them. From the entryway, the living room lit up brightly, too bright, in contrast to the darkness outside, and

Alec squinted. He helped Daisie to the foot of the stairs, but by the base of the stairway, he nearly dropped her when she closed her eyes and fell completely limp.

"Where are you taking her?" Joy asked.

"To the bedroom."

"Why? Just take her to the couch in the living room. She's already out cold in your arms. Don't take her upstairs."

"I know, but the only bed in my house is in the bedroom."

"So? Look, my inebriated friend, you're going to drop her if you lift her up all these steps. You don't want my help, fine, but why the hell does she get to sleep in your bed?"

"Does it matter?"

Then he froze looking at her. Because she met his gaze with those eyes. It was so mesmerizing.

"Hey, wait a second," he said, "didn't you leave your car back in Badger? How are you going to get your car back?"

"It's a small town. I can hitch a ride. Or walk. It's a half day's journey by foot. I've done it many times at this time of the year. Don't worry about me, worry about you. Like, how the hell are we going to get this sloshed, unconscious guest up into your bedroom? Wouldn't it be a whole lot easier if you dragged her to the sofa? Can't we do that instead, Alec?"

That's when he looked down and noticed Joy's bare feet. They went in and out of focus as he stared at them on the white carpet. Did she ever wear shoes? And, if not, and she had been walking in the forest, why did her feet seem so perfectly clean? It was really weird.

She lifted her brow, still waiting for an answer.

"*Hey!*" Daisie suddenly jarred awake, opening her eyes wide in Alec's arms. "Hey, wait one second! Wait just one second. Ain't there a fu-gg-in' ghost in this house!" And that sent her barreling into more laughter than ever. "You, you, you tryin' to scare the shit out of me on the Fourth of July, Alec? It's the Fourth of July, not Halloween. I said take me home, mister. Home. My home. You take me home this instant. It's not—"She looked up into his eyes and suddenly feigned being coy—" well, it's not proper, you know, for a girl to be sent here when she's not herself. Take me back home or I'll climb down the hillside, trees and bushes or not, and go home myself."

"Daisie, I'm trying to help you. Why not just rest until tomorrow?"

"I say let her crawl down the hill," Joy quipped. "You wouldn't want to take advantage of her."

"What?" Alec snapped, looking back. Joy just shrugged with a smirk. "Look, can you help me get her upstairs?"

Joy frowned.

"Who are you talking to, Alec?" asked Daisie. "Is there somebody else in the house? I like you and all, I really do, I mean, you're so cute with that tight black shirt over your chest and arms." She laughed. "But, but, but, but inside I think you can be a bit looney. Sometimes. And…you know…you know what, I tell you what. I told you, I love that. I really do. I told you… I really love that a lot. You know what I'm gonna do because of that? I tell you what I am going to do. I'm gonna give you a free reading. You know, I'm really good with tarot. Would you like your future read from my tarot cards? A free reading? I think—" She suddenly opened her eyes wide and turned from him— "uh, oh."

"Joy, please!" said Alec. "Please help me get her up to the bathroom upstairs!"

"What's so goddamn joyful about this?" Daisie snapped, groaning.

"Take her back to the powder room near the kitchen, dummy!" Joy cried.

"How do you know there's a powder room by the kitchen?" he asked. "There you go again. Why am I thinking you've been in this house a lot more than just that one time?"

"What?" asked Daisie, barely opening her eyes. "What the hell are you talking about. I don't see how many…uh, oh. Here I go again."

Daisie opened her eyes wide. And then, it was too late. She threw up all over the carpet steps.

"Goddamn it, Alec," Joy snapped. "You're too drunk to think straight."

And Daisie didn't stop throwing up. She crouched over the carpet on the two bottom steps, vomiting everywhere while Alec held her.

Then, finally, she wiped her mouth.

"There," Daisie said. "Done."

That made Joy burst into laughter.

"It's not funny," Alec said.

"*Fu-nn-y?*" Daisie drawled, wiping her mouth. "This is hardly funny, Alec." But then she chuckled.

"I think she's very funny," Joy said, still laughing. "Don't worry about the carpet. I'll clean it up. It was worth it to watch that."

"You know, I feel a little better now," Daisie said, clutching Alec's arm. "But, God, it's like the walls are still spinning around and around. Why did I drink so much? I mean, why? Maybe I should go see a doctor."

"Normie?" Joy asked, still laughing. "Man, you are drunk, Daisie."

"Stop it, Joy." Alec cried in a forced whisper. "Please. Stop laughing."

"Joy?" Daisie said. "There's nothing… Wait, God, I'm sorry for yelling at you. I just feel…don't feel good, Alec."

"Just rest," said Alec. "Forget it. You'll be all right."

"You're so sweet," Daisie said dreamily, looking into his eyes.

"Now *I'm* gonna throw up," Joy quipped.

"We need to take you to bed," Alec said.

"But I'll need help changing, Alec," Daisie said. "I threw up all over my dress. I can't get in your bed like this. I'll have to change into different clothes before I get in your bed."

Then she looked up at him with a large smile.

"Course not." Joy rolled her eyes. "Wouldn't want her dirty tits and ass smearing up your bedsheets."

"Joy!"

"Why do you keep saying joy?" asked Daisie.

"I'll help her get undressed and into bed," Joy said, rolling her eyes.

"Thanks so much, Joy. You're being so nice to us."

Daisie looked up at him squinting her eyes. She shook her head. Then she held back a burp and guffawed in his face.

ORANGE JUICE

One of Alec's greatest surprises in his house was the fact that the lake's horizon was to the east. Facing east meant that when dawn broke, beautiful yellow and orange rays of sunlight would reflect off the large body of water and slowly make their way over the trees on the horizon. And his long balcony afforded the brilliant view. It's one of the features that motivated him to get up early. That's what he was doing now. He got up before sunrise and walked down his long terrace to sit on a white plastic chair and watch the perfect view, waiting for sunrise. And while waiting in darkness, on his computer screen, he typed:

Nothing…

Absolutely nothing. He just stared at a blank screen.

He had only written twenty pages in the past month. The reality versus the dream of living in nowhere was settling in. He found that Plymouth Crest was too beautiful. Or was it his anxiety over the fact that he might not be here much longer? His realtor friend had still not gotten any leads. That was good and bad news. At the moment, that dunce Robin couldn't evict him, but it made his future very uncertain.

The horizon brightened and glowed orange. Then over the trees across the lake rose a single yellow dot. The sun. And the sun got bigger and brighter rising over the water. Wisps of clouds glowed the same red orange as the reflections of sunrays upon the lake. As the sun finally rose, the whole landscape turned a bright yellow.

Alec put on his shades and just leaned back in his chair watching. *Sighing*… Yeah, this was why he couldn't write.

He heard a bird flutter in the trees. It seemed to be at the crest of an elm. Otherwise, it was quiet enough to hear leaves flutter in the wind.

That's when he spotted someone standing below the terrace near his cement patio. She was so quiet that, for all he knew, she could have been standing under him since he got up this morning. As before, she wore her black shawl over her shoulders, a dark blouse and jeans, with her arms wrapped around herself. And she just stared out at the lake wearing sunglasses too.

"Joy," he hollered. "Joy. Hey, Joy!"

She cocked her head up and waved dismissively. Then she turned back, wrapped her arms around herself again, swayed a bit, and continued to watch the sun rise.

"Joy," said Alec, standing up and waving at her. "Joy. What are you doing down there?"

"Same thing you're doing, ding-a-ling," she answered with a smile. "Enjoying the sunrise. Do you know what's cool about sunrises over the lake, Alec? You get two for one up here off Plymouth Crest. Two. One reflected on the lake and another in the sky."

And they laughed.

"Come inside," he said. "I want to thank you for all your help the other night."

She walked right below the terrace. Then she looked up and smiled.

"Great weather we're having?"

"Is that small talk I hear?" Joy asked, tipping down her shades. "Small talk doesn't suit you. You are the least inauthentic man I've ever met."

"Oh, I just wanted to say something. Thanks so much for everything you did for us on the Fourth. What you did for Daisie was amazing. I'm so grateful. Did you get your car back?"

"Sure, it was nothing," she said with a nod. But then she cocked her head back at the sunrise. "The lake is so pretty, isn't it?"

Yes, Joy, sure is.

"Do you want to come up to my balcony?" Alec asked. "It's an even better view up here."

"Are you actually inviting me inside your home?" Joy asked with a smirk, bringing her shades down her nose a bit. "My, how things change."

"Yes. I… I can make you a cup of coffee?"

"I don't drink coffee."

"How about tea?"

"I learned long ago to avoid stimulants."

"How about orange juice?"

She turned back to the view, of course. Then she just gazed out quietly. Looking down at her, Alec wasn't sure which vision was more beautiful.

"Well?" he asked. "How about it? Orange juice?"

"Whatcha writing?" she asked, turning to him again.

"It's dead."

"You're writing about someone dead?"

"Uh…no. It's just an idea."

"What?"

"Nothing."

"Tell me. I want to know."

"It's just a story."

"About…" She gesticulated with one hand.

"Well, it's a book about a couple in St. Louis. The young couple meet each other on a train. He works in sales for a pharmaceutical company. She's a doctor. They talk about this new medicine being developed by a big Pharma company. Then they do the usual: fight bad guys. Well, the twist…you don't really want to know all this, do you?"

"Why wouldn't I?"

"It's just a story. You want to come up to my balcony and watch the sunrise with me?"

"No. I hate balconies. I tell you what, I'll take you up on orange juice—only if you tell me more about your story in St. Louis. I love stories, particularly love stories. Okay Alec, I'm coming through the kitchen door to get orange juice, but you best not throw the kitchen door in my face again."

"I won't," he said with a chuckle.

Alec laid his computer down on the cement under the chair. Then he bounded across his bedroom and down the stairs.

Along the inside balcony, he could see the bright sun was just starting to shine through the living room, and with all the windows, it was brightening the whole house. He made it to the kitchen before her, snatched two glasses, and poured some juice. And then he just sat down at his small circular dining table and stared at the door, waiting and catching his breath.

Joy arrived, still wearing shades, knocking on the glass of the kitchen door. When Alec opened the door, she reached out for a friendly hug. They embraced. She had this wonderful scent. He couldn't place the perfume, but he recalled smelling it in his car. It was a natural rose scent.

Then Alec squinted at her bare feet.

"Shoes are confining," she said with a chuckle and

shrug. She walked to the kitchen table and plopped down on a chair. "This juice better be good, Alec." She removed her sunglasses. "I'm missing an amazing sunrise by our lake. My favorite thing is to watch the sunrise every morning here on Plymouth Crest, Alec. I absolutely love it. It's so pretty, isn't it?"

"You're funny, Joy."

"Am I? Friends always say I'm funny. Cause…you know, I'm full of *joy*. Get it. *Joy?* That's my name." And she grinned, picked up the orange juice, and toasted him. "Um, yummy."

But then they sat across from each other, gazing at one another, and falling into an uncomfortable silence.

"Where do you live?" he finally blurted.

She shook her head before sipping more juice.

"Me first," she said. "Tell me about this story about a couple in St. Louis. Why'd you call the story *"dead"*? *Dead* is so fascinating in such a grim, dark, and dreary sort of way."

"No, I meant I have writer's block. I can't figure out what to write. The idea was to talk about doctors and the pandemic, maybe bring out a connection with a patient the two lovers knew who died. I wanted to address all the post-pandemic angst. Maybe talk about how they find something that's tainted that the industry's selling. You know how there are so many conspiracies these days."

"You don't know what's going to happen next? No wonder you've got writer's block. You sort of should know what you're writing about before you write stuff."

"I have ideas."

"Ideas aren't enough. I knew this writer who used to outline from start to finish. She'd go through, like, four sheets of paper crossing stuff out with a red pen and planning everything. She was so organized. She always had the ending on the last page. She knew exactly where her story was going. So—"

"I never outline. But, no offense, what do you know about writing?"

"I know movies," she said with a shrug. "And I read lots of stuff."

She looked up for a second and smiled. He adored her smile. Then she put a finger to her chin, still looking up pensively. Those brilliant blue eyes were so pretty and alluring. It was electrifying when she gazed back at him.

"A couple meets on a train?" she asked. "Hmm... I'm guessing they're, like, sitting in separate rows and one is passing the complimentary lunch of the day to the other across the aisle or something. Maybe a plastic fork or knife falls on a lap?"

"You've never been on a train, have you?"

"Hey, what's that supposed to mean?"

But she sipped more orange juice.

"There are dining cars in trains," he said. "You get up and go to the dining car to order food for yourself. That's been my experience when I used to ride trains in the Midwest. Unless it's super expensive. Then, I think, you could pass a plate, I suppose, but I wouldn't know. I've never been on an expensive train before."

"Right, well, I've never traveled on a train, smarty. But I know dining cars. Seen them in the movies. All right. So..."

She put a finger to her chin and looked up again. She brushed her long dark hair back. Alec was taken by that. Just watching her run her fingers through her hair.

Looking back, her lips curled into a wry smile. "What?"

"Nothing," he said. "Why are you trying to help me, Joy?"

"I love, love stories. Okay, so, shh, stop interrupting me. Let me think." She looked up in thought again. "I'm here to help—since you don't have any idea what you're writing about."

She chuckled.

But then she sipped more juice. She wiped her lips with the back of her hand.

"You want some tea?" Alec asked.

"No, already. Shush. Don't interrupt. Let me think… okay, so they're both on a train riding through St. Louis, past that arch and stuff. Seen the arch a lot too. Well, maybe they meet in line at the dining car. So in the dining car he orders Cheetos—oh my God, Alec, I frickin' love Cheetos, especially red hot Cheetos, they're so good—but she orders Doritos." She laughed and it made him laugh too. "No accounting for taste. I mean, Doritos are amazing too, particularly Ranch Doritos. Anyway, she opens the chip bag because she's starving to death. Because she's a doctor and doctors are always working and don't have enough time to eat. She didn't have time to get breakfast. Right? But that makes some of the chips fly out of her bag and hit him in the face. How's that? Then they'll be like:

"Excuse me," Joy said in a different accent. *"How embar-rassing."*

"No problem," Joy said in a lower voice.

Then he'll pick up one of the Cheetos that fell on her shirt collar and throw it in his mouth.

"I like Cheetos too," he'll say.

"See, then that strikes up a conversation about health food and how unhealthy their breakfast chips are, though they both love their bag of chips. And it leads to talking about vitamins and other boring doctor things—you'd have to look those things up, Alec. That author I was telling you about, she wouldn't even have started page one without already having looked stuff up. Anyway, this leads to talking about medicine. That leads to Covid. And they talk about how they didn't do much during the pandemic except drive to and from work. And that opens up the woman to finally being asked her name.

"What are we naming the doctor?"

Joy stopped talking and took another quick sip of the orange juice. But, after a silence, she gestured with both hands for him to answer.

"Elvira."

"Elvira?" she asked, scrunching her nose. "Eww. That's an awful name." But then her lips curled into one of her wonderful smiles. "Oh, *Elvira*. You're thinking, like, Elvira, the lady of the night? She was so very witchy, Alec. I loved her so much. Like vampires and ghouls movie host Elvira. I frickin' loved Elvira when she used to host scary movies. She was so funny. Did you ever see her when 3D movies were the rage? Remember those red and blue glasses? Those were such fun flicks. Okay. Well, Elvira would ask the guy what he does next, right?"

"I wasn't thinking of that Elvira. I just thought the woman would be named Elvira."

"Whatever. So they meander back to their seats, eating chips for breakfast, talking about the pandemic and their jobs as a doctor and a medical equipment salesman. Chip —we can call him Chip, cause of all this chip stuff I've been thinking about."

Alec frowned. And he felt all his excitement leave him.

"What the hell's the matter?" she asked. "Did I say something wrong?"

"Chip is the name of my best friend—my best friend who just ripped me off for this house. If he can't fix things, I'll be forced to leave."

"Wow, what the hell happened?"

"You don't want to help with my story anymore?"

"Not if something's really bothering you. If something's bothering you, Alec, I'd rather talk about that."

"Chip was my roommate in college. He sold me this

place, but I recently found out that the place might not be mine. Turns out, the man who sold me the house didn't own it. It was some kid who believed he could sell the house without properly transferring the title. You were right. The purchase agreement was a sham—not sure how you knew…"

She shrugged.

"Well, apparently, the real owner is either some pop star who might have passed away here, or this guy, Fifi's agent, who skipped town and nobody knows where he is."

She sipped more orange juice and nodded. But then she quickly put the glass down because her hand had started to shake.

"You all right?"

"Diabetes, I think. Too much juice—"

"You've barely drank any." Her glass was still completely full. She was, oddly, sipping very little of it. It seemed she had hardly drunk any.

"Doesn't take much for me."

"Maybe I shouldn't have given you the juice?"

"I absolutely love drinking orange juice with you, Alec. This is totally worth it. Never mind. What are you going to do?"

"I don't know why I'm telling you about all this," he said, shaking his head. "You make me feel comfortable, I guess, Joy. You know something funny? For a while, I actually thought *you* might be Fifi Graynger's ghost."

"That's funny," she said with a laugh.

He leaned back in his chair with a nod. Then he glanced through the glass in the kitchen door. "You're right, I made you miss the sunrise. Sorry."

"I'd rather spend my morning drinking orange juice with you. You make me feel comfortable too, Alec. But, never mind… God, how can I help you keep your house?

What the hell are you going to do? You love this place, don't you? How are you going to stay here?"

"Without escrow, I don't even know how or why I'm here. It cost me a fortune to move all my stuff in."

"Well, until you know, I think you should just carry on." She tapped her juice glass with red fingernails. "Don't worry about owning things. You know, everyone gets so hung up on owning stuff. Even if you received title and owned the house, Alec, you'd only have it for a few years. Maybe a decade? Most people move out of their house within five years or less. Nothing is permanent. Except the important stuff. Like our lake. Like the sunrise. If there's one thing I've learned from my life, it's that there's nothing permanent in this world. We all live and die. That was a mistake I once made. But the lake, like God, lives on. God's always with us, Alec. So, you know, why not just enjoy the sunrise? You know, enjoy your life. Forget the paperwork. Enjoy the lake. That's permanent. And the forest. That's why you left your job in California, right? To forget about all of this stuff. What did you say you retired from?"

"I never told you I retired," he answered, feeling suspicious of her again. "I was an accountant."

"What brought you here to Plymouth Crest?"

He raised his hand as she brought more juice up to her lips.

"If you have diabetes, stop drinking it, Joy."

"No. So, what brought you to Plymouth Crest? To nowhere land? You obviously love this lake and forest as much as me."

"I suppose I wanted to turn the page. My wife passed away a few years ago."

"God, I'm sorry."

"It wasn't unexpected. The worst was the years watching her suffer in pain. She died of breast cancer. She was young, only in her forties. But the treatment, I think, killed her. Yeah, it was so hard for my daughter Rachel and I. Very hard."

"I hear you talking to your daughter a lot. Or… I mean, at least, I heard the way you talked to her once and it was so nice. A true family is really special. My family was just me and my mom, but Mom was always working. Then she died when I was only a teenager."

"Well, you know——" And he looked into her eyes, loving them again.——"my wife's death taught me life is short. I learned I had to live life now. I suppose I did a little living with my own business as a CPA back in California, but my writer side wanted more. I wanted to live somewhere quiet to just do what I really love. Writing. That's all, I suppose. And now I'm here. The only thing I miss a lot is my daughter, Rachel."

"Well, you found quiet," she said with a nod. Then she lifted her orange juice glass, as if in a toast. "Hmm. I say… don't overthink things, Alec. Here's to Plymouth Crest. While you live in this house, I say live in the house. You needn't worry, like an accountant. This house has been abandoned for decades. So I say, enjoy it. It's yours."

"I wish things were that simple, Joy."

"They are. You believe something is yours, it's yours. I got stuck in a dream once. Got everything I ever wanted, but I was miserable. You know, with all my wealth, I never really was able to keep a thing. I moved here. Just like you. I thought it was temporary. Everything is temporary. But you know what I discovered? The sun always rises and sets. See, God is always here."

"What was your dream, Joy?"

She got up and walked over to the glass door pensively. Then she shook her head slowly, staring out at the trees.

"I spend most of my time outdoors now," she said. "I think, Alec, I don't really like the indoors anymore." She leaned her head on the glass. "But I love Plymouth Crest, and the forest and the lake are all I really need to feel happy. Things aren't so bad, I guess, if I'm here. It's so beautiful, and that's all that really mattered. Just enjoy what you have. The moment. Don't try to make it something it isn't. Don't overthink things. Just enjoy what you see and feel in your life."

"You're beautiful."

"What?" She spun around with a smile.

"Nothing," he said, getting up. "Sorry to bring up my troubles to you."

"Hmm, I'm almost sure I heard you say something else. I just want you to be happy. Happiness comes from not worrying. It's really about not worrying about anything at all. That's the Zen way, you know."

"Well, I have to thank you," Alec said, standing beside her. "You helped me and my friend so much. You even cleaned the stairs. I was too drunk to—"

"Don't worry about all that. That's what I'm trying to tell you. Stop thinking and…you know, enjoy the sunrise and orange juice in the morning."

He nodded. Then he rose and walked closer to her. Their heads were only a foot apart. Her rose perfume permeated the air. And he felt as if he were in a trance staring down into those bright blue eyes. She gave him that grin he loved. Then he reached out to touch her hand, but she quickly jerked it away.

"I… I'm sorry," he said. "I didn't mean—"

She shook her head, seemingly upset for a moment. But then she shocked him by throwing her arms around him. He gasped in surprise and just stood frozen and locked in her embrace. He was afraid to say a word or even move, because he hoped she wouldn't move either. Because, for some reason—he couldn't put his finger on it —but for some reason he feared that if either of them moved, or spoke, this wonderful feeling would end. Just as she had said, if he thought about it too much, she would be gone.

"I wish I had met you a long time ago," she whispered in his ear. "You're wonderful. Thanks for the juice. You're such a good man. But now I've gotta go."

"What? Why so soon?" he asked, finally letting go. "Where? Aren't you going to tell me about yourself? Where do you live? I'll visit. Or…tell me why you love, love stories so much."

"How 'bout this one," she said, gently touching the doorknob. "I'm not a writer, but when I lived in L.A. I knew plenty of them. I'm also not originally from Plymouth Hill. We came from the same place. Los Angeles. And I came here for quiet too. You and I have a lot in common, I think. We seem to like the same things. Except accounting. Eww, I could never do math."

"When can we meet again?" he asked at the door. "Maybe we can go together to Badger."

"Badger?" She wrinkled her nose. "Eww, gross. You kidding me? Not much to do in Badger. It's really no different than here. If you stay around Plymouth Hill long enough, you'll learn there's nothing to do for hundreds of miles except enjoy the outdoors. That's why I'm here. I love it. How about we just take a walk together one morning?"

"All right. How about tomorrow morning?"

"Alec." She laughed. "Okay. I guess. I can knock on your door tomorrow morning. Sound good?"

"Just no breaking and entering."

"I'll knock. I promise."

Joy opened the kitchen door.

As she turned a corner around a wide tree, right before disappearing in the green overgrowth, Alec waved and said, "You can break in again anytime, Joy."

She waved back at him.

What are you doing, Alec? Are you falling for her?

Yes, he had that feeling in his chest again. That same feeling he had when he moved into the house. *Joy*.

Joy reappeared in an opening between more trees. She was walking so calmly and serenely. But as she passed another tree down the hill, she dipped her head, smiled, and waved.

"Can't wait, Alec," she said.

She was so lovely. So vibrant. So alluring.

But then he felt shock. Maybe she really was Fifi Graynger, the pop star? Had Fifi been hiding all this time in Plymouth Hill pretending to have died? She certainly was attractive enough and had that enchanting singing voice. Perhaps she had come here to escape the world, just like he had.

He took his cellphone from his pants pocket and searched the internet for Fifi Graynger. He had glanced at her image before but had never thought to compare her with Joy. No. In this image, Fifi held a microphone, singing to thousands of fans on an outdoor stage. The pop star's facial features were completely different from Joy's. Her skin wasn't as smooth as Joy's, and her hair was dirty blond and in braids, not black. Joy definitely didn't look like her. The only resemblance was the singer's age. And, if possible, Joy was actually even prettier.

He chuckled and shook his head.

BE WITH ME

ALEC WOKE UP STARING AT THE CEILING. HE WAS AMAZED he had dozed off at all after tossing and turning, his mind buzzing. He couldn't stop obsessing over the house he was now worried he'd lose. He wanted the place so badly. Maybe he had fallen asleep because of the lack of noise? The slamming of cabinets and doors and the footsteps had mysteriously disappeared last night. Now it seemed almost too quiet.

But his mind wandered again...

Was it over thoughts of the house or was it over Joy? Was he falling for her? He felt that same "crush" he'd felt so many times before, kind of like his crush on the greatest love of his life, his late wife. But was it love or curiosity? She seemed so odd. Maybe the unknown was what drew her to him?

No. Joy was truly the most beautiful woman he had ever seen, sure, but he was so much older than she was. And he still knew so little about her. She had intelligent eyes. She was smart, caring, and kind. And funny... She was very funny. Yes, she was perfect, as alluring as the house itself.

But she was so strange. Perhaps she lived in the forest? Then how did her clothes and her appearance always appear so well kept?

They hadn't kissed on the lips in the kitchen, but they had embraced for such a long time. Somehow, that had felt so much better.

No, it wasn't just suffering from insomnia over losing the house now, it was restless thoughts over Joy.

He turned to look at his clock beside his bed. It read two-thirty in the morning in digital red letters.

A gust of wind picked up outside. Trees swayed with the sound of rain pelting hard on the ground. Rain in July? Only in Plymouth Hill.

Then a flash of lightning lit up his entire bedroom.

He jumped. He wasn't alone in the room. Standing by the glass door before the terrace, in front of red velvet drapes shifting from a breeze that, queerly, was blowing inside the bedroom, stood a lady wearing a translucent white silk nightgown. By moonlight, he could make out the curves of her breasts and hips through the thin garment. But she was paying absolutely no attention to him. She was so quiet, it seemed she could have been standing there while he had slept for hours.

"Who's there?" Alec asked.

"Don't go."

The words didn't seem to come from the woman. They were whispered all around the room. And yet, it sounded like Joy's voice.

There was another flash of lightning. And she disappeared.

Thunder shook the whole room.

Alec jumped as someone, or some thing, appeared on his bed. She straddled him and he fell back in shock against his pillow. It was his lady by the lake. It was Joy! He couldn't fully discern her face in the darkness, but he smelled that familiar rose perfume. Her eyes, in the shadows, peered into his. She gently ran her hand through his thin beard and short hair while staring into his eyes.

"What's going on, Joy?"

"Shh, stop thinking, Alec," Joy whispered. She ran kisses along his neck, and then he finally felt what he had desired in the kitchen when they embraced—the gentle touch of her lips. "Please. Stop thinking or it will be over. Enjoy this night with me. You're sleeping."

He gazed at her breasts and along the curve of her stomach to her legs, through the translucent silk nightgown. She watched him undress her. Then she leaned down again and ran her lips along his beard. He heard their kisses as they made out. Then he felt fingers ran along his hair again, massaging his head, hearing her breathing grow heavier. All the while, she kept shifting weight down, moving along his underwear and over the bulge from his cock, arousing him more.

"You're so attractive," she whispered by his ear. But that's what he had been thinking about her.

She squeezed him tight. Then she sat up tall, lifting her nightgown over her shoulders, revealing her soft breasts in the shadows of the moonlight.

"Joy!" he gasped.

"Shh," she whispered. "Be calm or this will be over. Do you want this to end, Alec? Just relax and don't worry. If you worry, you'll wake up from the dream and we can't do this."

"Am I sleeping?"

"Shhh. Yes. I told you you're asleep. This is the only way."

She gently ran her fingers through his beard. Then she shifted to his side and ran her hand along his legs.

"I wanted you in the kitchen so badly," she said quietly. "Shhh," she whispered in his ear. "Just rest. Now, I can feel you, only if you rest and allow me to. Do you want me, like I want you? I can leave you be to sleep if you want. I wish you would sleep better. You're always tossing and turning."

She leaned down and kissed his lips again. Then they were at it again, making out while he stroked her soft breasts, running his fingers over her nipples.

"Do you want to make love to me, Alec?" she whispered.

"Yes."

She gently took his fingers in hers and ran his hands along her soft breasts again. Their hands explored each other's bodies together, as she lay over him, gently rocking over his hard cock. She moaned. He felt so aroused. He pressed his fingers into her back, massaging her, then pressed along her shoulder blades. Gently, she guided his hands slowly down again, along her lower back, and then over the crack of her ass. All the while, she kept gently rocking over him.

"Joy…how did you appear and—"

"Shh, still your mind. Don't think, Alec, or it all could end."

As she sent more kisses along his neck, he answered by pulling down his underwear. And, before he knew it, he was inside her.

Another flash of lightning revealed her nakedness as she straddled him. She was sitting up, presenting her perfect body as she moved up and down over him. Thunder rumbled. And more flashes came, illuminating the room and their bodies, as bright as day. She grasped his hands in hers again, massaging them and bringing each finger up to her lips to kiss and suck. She seemed so focused on his hands. Every finger seemed to be more important than his body. Then she moaned as she grasped them tightly.

Darkness returned and, for a moment, it seemed as if

her body had disappeared. Alec could only hear the sound of their lovemaking, still feeling her weight rock over him, which was just as alluring.

Lightning flashed. She appeared again in the shadows, staring into his eyes. That was wonderful—just gazing deeply into her eyes.

Then came another rumble of thunder.

"Is this really happening?"

"Yes," she whispered. "Don't think. Feel. If you think, it will all be over. We can only do this while you're sleeping. Oh, I've watched you and wanted to touch you like this for so long. Dance with me. Touch me. If you think, you might… Oh, that's it…you might…just ruin everything. Stay calm and serene and just be with me. If you only knew how alone I've felt for so long. Be with me, Alec. Be with me. You feel absolutely wonderful."

He threw her on her back making her gasp in surprise. But then she laughed. He adored her laughter so much. Her eyes widened as he lay on top of her. He couldn't make out the blue, but he could see them open and hungry. He brushed his hand along her soft cheek and then reached down kissing her lips again, running his tongue along hers. Then he pressed deeper into her body, and she moaned more loudly as she ran her fingers through his beard and over his arms and chest. All the while, in the shadows of moonlight, as he pushed, she gazed deeply into his eyes.

Another lightning strike lit up her eyes like sapphires.

"Yes. That's it. Please, touch me. Touch me and… fuck me."

All turned dark as the entire room shook. It was not just thunder—it was as if an earthquake had rumbled the bed and the entire foundation of the house. He ran his fingers over her butt, squeezing her ass and pressing down over her harder. All the while she kept stroking his back and arms.

"That's it. Yes, Alec. Oh, please stay with me. Please!

Please be with me. Don't go. Oh, God, if you only knew how lonely I've been! I just want to touch and feel you forever!"

She took a deep breath and then fell limp under him. And he orgasmed with his weight over her. Then she caught him tightly in her arms and ran kisses along his neck and over his lips.

"Is this just a dream?" he asked, panting. "It seems so real."

"Can I stay in your arms while you sleep? I can help you…stay asleep, if you want. For a little while, if it's what you want, Alec. Then I can be in your arms longer. Do you want that? I'd love that so much."

"Yes."

"While you sleep, I can lie in your arms and finally touch you with my hands." He felt her running her hands along his back again, then over his hands, stroking his fingers again. "Lie with me, Alec. Lie with me."

They lay on their sides, staring into each other's eyes. He ran his hands along her back, pressing against her soft hips and breasts as she kissed him again gently on the cheek and lips.

"I want to touch you for as long as I can. I wish I could forever."

"It is a dream."

~

He awoke staring up at the ceiling again. Then he heaved a sigh. How could it not have been a dream? Joy wasn't in his room. How could she be?

But whatever it was, it was amazing.

"Don't go."

SEARCHING FOR JOY

EVER SINCE MIDNIGHT, WHEN HE AWOKE FROM HIS VIVID and unsettling wet dream, rain had continued to fall in a tempest of fierce winds, throwing branches and trees against the walls of his house, blowing away anything he had laid outside—chairs, vases, tables—right down the hill-side and into the woods below. The wind was so powerful that it tossed his plastic chair right off the terrace. It had rained so hard that there was about a foot of water surrounding the foundation. *Well, there goes my walk this morning with Joy.*

Alec ventured downstairs, walking along the mezzanine, marveling at the inside of his home. Though it stormed outside, and he was surrounded by the sight of the outdoors, he was still warm and cozy. He loved his house so much. He headed to the kitchen to brew coffee.

That's when his cellphone rang from the bedroom.

So back he went, bounding upstairs and around the indoor balcony and running inside his bedroom to not miss the call.

"Yeah," he clambered, panting.

"Hey, man," Chip said.

"Do you have any idea what time it is, Chip? And… isn't it like three in the morning in Los Angeles?"

"Yep. Three in the morning. But six o'clock in Costa Rica. I told you I'd make things better. I found the owner. Or at least someone just as good, better than Robin."

"Really?" Alec asked, walking back down the stairs. "I don't know whether to kiss you or smack you in the face."

"Kiss me, buddy. Reggie's alive and well. He's not officially the owner, but he's got a better chance of taking possession of the place than his son. And here's the kicker. He doesn't give a shit about it, Alec. In fact, it's possible I can shave off more from the sale. He was in shock when I told him about it. He was led to believe the place burned down decades ago. All he wants is the money."

"His son didn't talk to him about it?"

"I don't think he's speaking to his son."

"What's the catch?"

"Why do you always think there's a catch, man? Well, time. I need to fax a ton of documents to the guy and wait for him to work things out. I might even have to take a vacation in Costa Rica. Could be worse, right? But at least this guy, unlike our music star, is alive and well. Really, the only catch is me. If I talk down the price, I get less of a cut for our sale."

"Fuck you, Chip."

"Yeah, I deserved that. Now"—He yawned—"I've really gotta get some rest. It's frickin' three o'clock in the morning here. I'll get everything arranged. I've arranged another phone meeting with Reggie later. He wanted to meet early. Now that there's a big deal for him, he wants to chat again. So I'll find out more soon enough and call you back. Don't worry. When everything's ready, I'll fax the papers back to you. Unless you want me to come by your house again? Please say you don't want me to travel back to Plymouth Hill, Alec."

"Email," Alec said with a chuckle. "But God knows where a fax machine is around here."

"Email can turn into faxing, genius. What century were you born in? Man, you really belong there in the middle of nowhere."

"Has he been the one forging Fifi's name?"

"No. I wondered about that. He said he wasn't sure, but he was certain it wasn't Fifi. He said he witnessed her death. I still haven't solved that riddle yet, but I will. Like I said, at least now I have a lead I can talk to, not some dead pop star."

"Fix it and get me the papers to sign the house over."

"Sure thing, buddy. Will do."

"Bye, Chip."

"Bye."

Alec hung up the cellphone. Then he just walked over to a lounge chair in the living room and gazed over his left shoulder at the outside. The rain was picking up again, and there was a wall of water outside the window now.

There goes my date.

He fell back in his chair. Did it matter? If he wasn't leaving Plymouth Crest, neither was Joy. There'd be plenty of chances to walk with her later.

Alec woke to knocking. Had he fallen back asleep?

Was it Joy!?

The thought was enough to stir him and make him rush to the front door. He still had his phone in his pajamas pocket. It read eight o'clock. It was still pouring rain outside.

He gazed through the peephole. Nope, it was Daisie. Daisie stood under the overhang by the front patio wearing a long red coat and matching beret. Her red hair made her clothes appear darker, like burgundy. Behind her fell a wall of water. And Daisie's coat was sopping wet.

"Hey, Alec!" Daisie said, walking inside. She took her coat and hat off and he grabbed them. Then she gave him a quick hug. She glanced around the house and scrunched her nose. "Hey ghosts, any of you creepin' round the house?"

Then she did what everyone did after walking into his home. She headed into his amazing central living room. Her eyes surveyed the upstairs balcony and all the windows.

"You know, last time I was here, a group of my friends smoked cloves by your fireplace in the middle of the night."

Alec looked outside the still-open door. Visibility in the downpour was terrible. He imagined Joy might be out there somewhere. But why would she walk in this storm? She'd definitely be indoors this morning. Where—that was the real mystery.

As Alec turned back to Daisie, she presented him a gold wrapped box with a red bow. She must have been carrying it under the coat. It was the only thing that was dry.

"What's this?"

"Special *Daisie* delivery. Amazon doesn't deliver in Plymouth Hill, you know, so we make do round here."

"Yeah, but what is it?"

"Open it, silly."

Alec opened the gold wrapper. Inside was a box with an image of a flashlight with a bright beam of light.

"That is the amazing one I was talking about. Remember I couldn't find it? Well, I had to order it. They say that thing can shine light for a mile. I wouldn't be surprised if you can spot deer all the way down the hill by the lake in nighttime."

"I just needed a light for the house," he said with a chuckle.

"Yeah, well, it'll sure do that too."

"Thank you, Daisie."

A strike of lightning lit up the living room, making it as bright as day. It made the recess light on the ceiling seem dim.

"Love what you've done with the place," she said, ignoring the weather. But she couldn't ignore the thunder. It seemed to shake the entire foundation. She shook her head. "What a terrible storm. Even for Plymouth Hill. Your furniture is really modern, Alec. So L.A.. Really, not all that different from what was withering here years ago. Your stuff fits the place and looks really nice. The house has always been totally L.A., I suppose. I mean, with that indoor balcony, California chic totally fits your weird mansion."

She went straight over to the floor-to-ceiling window and just stared outside at the backyard.

"How are you liking our rain?" she asked, cocking her head back. "Get used to it. This is a July storm. Wait till you meet December flurries. Then the road shuts down in January, and you'll be landlocked for the new year. Might finally turn you totally *Shining* nutso. You know, you best be walking on the main road then anyway because black ice is treacherous for your fancy car. But…hmm, there's not much stuff outside on your patio."

"It was all blown away."

"See. That's what I'm talking about. Rain in Plymouth Hill."

Lightning flashed again. It made Daisie glow yellow near the window and the whole living room flash brightly for a moment. The light was on, but it seemed dimmer when the flash of light left. Then thunder shook the room and all the windows again. For a moment, the weather reminded him of his strange, vivid dream last night.

Daisie plopped herself on his black leather couch—

across from the chair he had been sleeping in—put her large leather purse on her lap, and just smirked at him. She wore a quarter moon on her forehead this time, but otherwise she seemed normal enough. And she wore a black sweater and dark slacks. She smelled nice, it was a strange mix of jasmine and mint.

She dug in her purse and took out a deck of cards. Then she laid the stack of cards on the coffee table before the couch.

"I owe you a reading. You were so nice to me on the fourth. You want to do your reading now? It'd be a lot of fun in this heavy storm."

He shrugged, sitting beside her.

"But you said you get up early, right?" Daisie asked, touching his leg. "Am I imposing?"

Only if Joy comes by.

Daisie shuffled the cards as if they were about to play poker.

"You want coffee?" Alec asked.

She shook her head. Then she started looking at a few of the cards.

"Isn't that cheating?"

"We're not gambling. These are tarot cards."

"How about orange juice?"

"No thanks. I hate orange juice."

"Okay, here," she said, moving the coffee table closer to them. Then she shuffled the cards, not looking this time. She took one card and pressed it against her forehead. "See this. Describe to me what the card looks like."

"The one covering your moon?"

"Uh, yeah," she chuckled. "Yeah. Describe it. Come on. It's your card, Alec. What does it look like?"

"It looks like a king carrying a grail."

"Oh, that's the king of cups. Yep. Wow. That sure fits you. It means you're sympathetic and kind. Artistic. A good listener. That's definitely you, Alec. Totally you. Now do you believe in the cards?"

Alec shook his head.

"Nonbeliever. Let's get to the good part. Let's see what your future holds."

Then she shuffled the cards again. She reached out to hold one of his hands. With the other hand, she kept moving the cards.

There was another strike of lightning. They squinted as the brightness rushed back into the living room. Then thunder quaked the glass windows.

"Jeesh, what an awful storm," she said. "But that could be good for my magical energy." She took one card, facing it down on the table. "Okay. Draw this one and show it to me."

There was another strike of lightning, and thunder that rocked the windows. But Daisie stared at Alec, waiting.

Alec flipped the card over. The card presented on the table was a guy on a throne. The bottom of the cartoon read "justice."

"An arcana card, Alec. Wow, an arcana. That's a goodie. Very good. Pull one more for your first reading. You need three for a reading. Three gives me the most information about your future."

"What does that card mean?"

"It means your life will be full of justice," she said with a nod.

He looked at her suspiciously.

"Do you know what you're doing?" he asked.

"What do you mean?" she asked, looking offended.

"Didn't you just read *justice* on the card?"

"I interpreted your king of cups, didn't I? Come on." She waved a hand at him dismissively and said, "Next card."

Alec chose a card with a cartoon of a naked couple

under a woman with wings. At the bottom of the card it said "lovers."

"Ah, another arcana card!" she said with a large grin. "How about that! Another arcana. I can't believe it. I love arcana cards. And this one's the best one." She winked. "Wow, Alec, how unusual. You picked the 'lovers' card. See. That's a special one. And that card means—"

Another flash of lightning lit up the living room. For a flash, again, it was as bright as day. But then a gale rushed *inside* the house, shaking the windows and blowing through the room, throwing Daisie's stack of tarot cards off the table.

But although it stormed outside, none of his windows were open.

Then the whole room shook with thunder, this time more violently than ever. It was almost as if there was an explosion. And a cold gale still blew against his face. Alec turned to the windows, thinking maybe one was open. Instead, a large vase barreled into the bushes amidst the whirlwind. And all the trees were swaying like crazy.

"Do you have a window open?" asked Daisie, staring at the windows too. "They all seem closed to me." She got on her knees and started picking up all the cards. "Or maybe the door's open? That's so weird."

Flash came another lightning strike. This one was so bright that it seemed to have hit the house. Thunder exploded again. That's when a woman appeared right outside the windows, drenched, holding herself in her arms. A yellow glow surrounded her, as if she weren't real but a part of the thunderbolt. The flash lasted just long enough for him to recognize her face. *Joy!* God, was Joy outside in the pouring rain? She stood out there glaring at them. She looked pissed. Alec jumped. But the minute he approached the window, Joy was gone.

"You best stand away from the windows," warned

Daisie. But she was on her knees, still gathering up all her cards from the carpet. "It sounds like the storm is right above your roof. You don't want to be struck by lightning." She looked up for a moment. "What the fuck happened? How the hell did the cards fly into the air *inside* your house, Alec? That is so weird."

Through the window Alec searched the woods for Joy. His small concrete patio was covered in a foot of water. But she wasn't there. Then he gazed farther up the hillside. No sign of Joy there either.

"Get that woman out of here," said a voice outside in a forced whisper. "Make her go. I mean it, Alec. Make her leave now!"

"Joy?"

"We're sure not having any joy if this storm keeps up, I'm afraid," quipped Daisie with a laugh. "Man, this is so bad. Good thing I drove. I was thinking of heading up the hill this morning. Walking would have been so stupid."

"You should probably stay until the storm lifts," commented Alec absentmindedly. He still searched the trees for Joy.

"*No!*" Joy cried.

Daisie threw a bunch of her cards on the table and then leapt up from her knees, rushing to the window. She searched the yard with him.

"You heard that?" he asked.

"Yeah." Daisie nodded, searching outside. "It sounded like a woman's voice outside shouting 'no.' Gosh, I hope there's no one out there right now in this terrible rain."

"I know a lady who keeps wandering outside. One of those drifters you were talking about."

"Well, she's stupid if she's outside of shelter in this storm. But I told you about them. I wasn't kidding. There are so many hikers and bohemians creeping about around this hill."

There was a bang. It wasn't thunder this time—it sounded more like a knock. It was coming from the kitchen. Then another gust of wind picked up *inside* the living room, and all of Daisie's collected tarot cards were tossed right off the table once more.

"What the hell is going on?" drawled Daisie with wide eyes. "Why is there wind *inside* your house, Alec. Alec… I… I think your house really is haunted."

"Wait a minute," he said, "I want to check around the house and make sure everything's okay. I'll be right back."

"Sure," Daisie said, with her eyes wide. "Sure, you do that. I'm not going anywhere." Because she was back to picking up her cards. "I don't believe this. This is wonderful, Alec. Your house is really frickin' haunted!"

"I'll be right back."

Alec rushed into the kitchen, where he had heard the knock. It was dark. The light switch didn't work. And there wasn't anyone there. Until another flash of lightning hit. Then, in the blinding white light, Joy stood shaking outside the glass kitchen door with her arms folded in pouring rain. When the lightning left, it turned very dark, but he could still see her standing outside. She wore a drenched dark blouse and jeans. Her dark hair was dripping wet too. And her eyeliner was runny. Drops of water fell from her face. But not only was she shivering, she was scowling.

He quickly opened the kitchen door.

"Let me—"

"Shh," Joy said in a whisper, shaking. "Shh, Alec. Shut up for a second. Be quiet." And she put a finger up to her lips. Then she looked toward the living room. The door was cracked open. She walked over and gently closed it. "Just be quiet for a sec," Joy said in a forced whisper. "Why is that woman here? Daisie's weird. And she's full of it. She knows as much magic as I do. She's just trying to seduce you."

"Go say hi to her, Joy," said Alec with a smile. "Come on. She'd love to meet you. You helped her on the Fourth, remember?"

"No," she said with a forced whisper. "Be quiet, I say. I don't want her knowing I'm here."

"Why? You helped her. Go say hi. You'd like Daisie."

"I don't want to right now. Not now. But you"—Her teeth chattered—"Hey, you promised to walk with me this morning."

"Seriously?" he asked incredulously, backing up. "You want to walk outside now?"

The funny thing was, though she was shivering and sopping wet, the idea of walking out in the pouring rain with Joy was the best proposition he had been given in years. She was all he had thought about since his dream.

Joy chuckled—but tried not to, covering her mouth, her body jerking. Then she laid a shaky finger over her lips.

"You're so cold," Alec said, searching all over the kitchen in the dark for a towel. "I'll find something to dry you."

A flash of lightning brightened the kitchen again. And then the house shook with another rumble of thunder.

"Alec," she whispered, "you invited me—remember?—to walk with you alone this morning. Not her. I knocked. Now get her the hell out of the house already."

"I'm ready," Daisie hollered from the other room. "I picked up all the cards. Unless that pesky ghost is going to mess them all up again." Daisie laughed. Joy narrowed her eyes. "You finished checking things over in your château, Alec?"

"Why the fuck do you think she came here this morning?" Joy snapped in a forced whisper. "Are you dense? She knows as much about tarot cards and witchcraft as you do. You can be so dense sometimes, Alec. Please make her go."

"But why?"

Joy threw her arms around him. He backed up, not because he objected to her embrace, but out of surprise. Her body was so wet and cold from the rain. But that made him squeeze her tighter in order to warm her. He felt the drops drip down all over him. A few drops even ran under his pajama shirt—he hadn't even had a chance to get dressed in regular clothes yet.

Then he felt her lips. Joy first kissed him gently. Then she pressed hard. And soon her lips were all over his beard and neck. He realized, though she had made love to him in his dream, this was their first real kiss. He had dreamt of being in her arms again, and now, even better, she was making out with him.

"This is why, mister," she whispered in his ear. "Okay? If you care about me like I do you, you'll honor this simple request for me this morning. Make her scram. No more questions. Just get that conniving witch to drive herself home. She'll be fine. She can drive straight down the hill to her store, but I don't want to see her right now."

"But…"

"But what?" She put a finger over her lips again. "No buts. Shh." Then she just looked deeply into his eyes. "Please, Alec. No questions. Stop thinking and do as I say."

Stop thinking…that's what she kept saying over and over in my dream.

She came closer to his ear and whispered, "This was supposed to be our morning. Remember? You invited me to come walk with you. Please don't be so nice to her that you hurt me."

"But we can't walk outside right now."

"We certainly cannot," said Daisie from the other room, laughing. "You can't expect to be walking outside in this rain, Alec. You're so crazy sometimes. Actually, I love that you're that crazy."

Thunder flashed again, lighting up the dark kitchen. Joy's eyes opened wide.

"Get her the fuck out now," Joy drawled in a whisper. Then she gnashed her teeth and raised her eyebrows. "She's not invited to join us. 'kay?"

Alec got out of her arms and rustled through drawers. All he had was a drawerful of small kitchen towels. He took the small towel out and presented it to her.

Joy rolled her eyes and snatched it. "Thanks."

"I'll stay," Joy whispered. "If she goes. But don't tell her I'm here. Please, Alec, please promise you won't tell her I'm here. Promise? Just figure out another excuse to have her go away."

"Let me at least get you a proper towel."

"Oh shit," Joy said, looking over Alec's shoulder. "Shit, shit she's coming! I'll just dry up in your powder room. Don't worry about me, worry about that witch. Get that witch the hell out of our house. You invited *me* this morning, remember? Not her. This…" She grimaced more deeply than ever and said quietly, with a country accent, "This town ain't big enough for the two of us, partner."

Then Joy ran to the nearby powder room and shut the door.

"Alec, you're so wet," said Daisie, opening the door from the living room. "Did you actually go outside in the storm? Are you crazy?"

"There's a lot of damage on the porch," Alec lied. Then he looked down at his bare feet standing in a pool of water. "I had to see if I could salvage some of my plants."

"Oh," Daisie said. But then she looked all around the dark kitchen. She switched on the light. The light switch worked this time. "I can't believe those cards were thrown off the table. We need to get a medium to check out this house—Luminous, or one of his friends. I'm only so good, you know. Most of my witchcraft comes from all the books

I read and tidbits here and there from wizards I've met. In the city, there's some real good ghost hunters that would frickin' love this place. Have you ever seen anything else move inside your house? That was unbelievable. It could be the lightning's stirring up just the right amount of paranormal energy for awesome stuff like that to happen. Have you been having any strange dreams in your house?"

Uh, yeah…

The lightning struck again. Then it shook the kitchen.

He heard a grunt come from the powder room.

He thought of her plea. Perhaps he should ignore it, stop the nonsense, and just have Joy come out and talk to Daisie? He didn't get it. She wasn't shy. Besides, didn't they know each other? They had to in such a small town. But disobeying her wishes seemed disrespectful.

And also…deep inside, Alec wanted to be alone with Joy too. And he felt like if he obeyed her, for whatever strange oddball reason—maybe she had social anxiety?—if he obeyed her request, they would still have their date.

But…*walk outside in pouring rain?* Daisie was right. That was crazy.

"Daisie, I'm expecting someone to be coming by the house any minute to do some really important business," Alec lied. "I so like your gift, but I was wondering if we could meet again later? Maybe I can come by later this afternoon or evening."

"Oh," Daisie said, furrowing her brow. "Sure. All right. You don't have to be so formal about it. I told you I didn't want to impose. This was sudden. Just got excited when I got the flashlight delivered last night."

"You haven't imposed. I really appreciate you stopping by."

"Sure. But…before I go, maybe we could try just one more reading? I'll shuffle the cards and—"

"You sure you'll be all right driving down the hill in the rain?"

"Sure," Daisie said. "Sure. No problem. Alec, you haven't been around here long enough. It's a bad storm but it's nothing compared with snow. I'm sorry if I imposed."

"You didn't. You're a great friend."

"You are too, Alec." She touched his shoulder and then looked around the kitchen. "Wow, you live in a real haunted house. This place is so awesome."

Alec reached to hug Daisie. There was another flash of lightning and the roar of thunder. The two embraced quickly in the kitchen, but Daisie kept her distance. Because Alec was soaking wet.

ETHEREAL

ALEC LEANED FORWARD, HEAD IN HANDS, ON THE BLACK leather lounge chair in his living room, waiting for Joy to take a shower upstairs. His dream last night had been so vivid. And now she had come back to him to take a morning walk together. During a thunderstorm. Things were getting weird…

He jumped up and walked up to the window, stroking his beard and staring outside. Of course, Joy was right. The trees weren't swaying anymore, the rain was drizzling, and the clouds were dispersing, revealing the bright golden sun. Yes, they could walk this morning, but they'd have to keep to muddy paths. If he was honest with himself, he was excited at the prospect of walking with her.

That dream had been so real—too real to be a dream. The only answer he could think of was simple: he was slipping into psychosis. That's what Daisie had warned him about. He was simply getting "cabin fever." But how long did it take to develop cabin fever? He had only been in Plymouth Crest for a few months. It hadn't even snowed yet.

"Ready?"

Joy stood at the base of the stairs looking very excited. He loved her energy. But, typical of her weirdness, she wore the same wet clothes she had worn in his kitchen. Still, despite a damp shirt and pants, her hair had been straightened and she looked, if possible, lovelier than before.

"Sorry," he stammered, "I should have offered to dry your clothes."

"Forget it. I'm warm enough, Alec."

She sauntered over and put her arms around him again. That spread dampness, but she wasn't cold this time. They gazed into each other's eyes again. Then he looked at her shoes—or lack thereof. Her feet were spotless. They were always so clean. Come to think of it, even when she had walked into the kitchen from the woods, they weren't dirty.

"Oh," she said, looking down. "Kinda weird about my feet. Do you want me to explain?"

"There's so much about you that's a mystery."

"Well, if you love something, can't it be ethereal?"

"Huh?"

"Well," she said with a shrug, "I mean, that is to say, if you like someone or something, someone, you know, that gives you joy, do you have to worry? Isn't everything in this world fleeting? That's what the Buddhists say. Everything changes. It's like the house. You were talking about losing it, but eventually we lose everything, don't we? Eventually, when you die, you have to give everything away. So, why can't we just enjoy the moment? What we touch, what we see, what we hear—does it always have to be attached to some desire? Can't we just enjoy the world God gave us?"

"Sure, I guess. That all sounds pretty deep to me."

"I think we can," she said, nodding pensively. Then she shrugged and chuckled. "Well, you're the writer, Alec."

She took two slow steps away from him but hesitated.

Then, with her back still turned, she reached out for his arm. "Shall we?" She hooked her arm around his, laughing happily again, and they passed over the threshold of his front door.

He had thought they'd head down the hill to the road by the lake, but she apparently intended the opposite. She headed uphill along a dirt path, now muddy, under a dripping wet canopy of branches and leaves that surrounded his backyard. He knew his grounds well enough to know where this trail headed: to an even higher lookout. Perhaps this peak was where she lived? Impossible. The pinnacle of the hill was just a small wild grassy knoll, hardly large enough for a home.

"I've been thinking more about your story," she said as they walked. "And I've got some ideas, if you'd like to hear them. Have you written anything else?"

"No."

"*Alec!*" she chided.

They turned up a steeper incline, up toward the summit of Plymouth Crest. And she held him closer.

"Well, why not have the couple meet on an airplane? Trains are so unfashionable these days. I was thinking you could turn the story into a destination novel. Wouldn't that be more exciting? They could meet on the way to Hawaii. Everyone loves Hawaii, right? The doctor could be sitting near the medical supply salesman on a plane. Or was he a pharmacist?"

"Medical supply. But the whole concept is a train, Joy."

"Well, hear me out. Maybe she's a new doctor and just hasn't had time to travel, but this is an exciting change. And he's getting out of some relationship and just wanted to let off some steam. He's single, so he figured he'd take a trip to the islands. Some people do that when they're lonely and single. Trust me, I should know. I did a couple jaunts myself back in the day. And, you know, if they're both going to a conference, Hawaii would be just the absolute perfect place. Wouldn't it?"

He shook his head.

"Why not?"

But he didn't answer. They just fell silent as they climbed.

Still, while his mouth didn't move, his thoughts were screaming. He couldn't stop wondering about her. Something seemed off. She had pristine bare feet, never with a blemish? He thought that maybe if he could solve that riddle, everything would become clear.

Is she the ghost of the house? Fifi's ghost?

She sure seemed like one last night.

But that was just a dream…wasn't it?

She seems as real as Daisie.

Was it possible a lady walked about everywhere barefoot? Didn't that cut up one's soles? Or did people get used to it? Cavemen didn't have shoes…did they?

"Hmm, Alec? How come you've gone quiet? What about Hawaii for your story instead of St. Louis?"

But what about her home? Where did she live? And if she was homeless, how come she always looked so clean and beautiful?

Because she's Fifi's ghost.

Impossible. Ghosts weren't real.

Her rose perfume permeated the air. That smelled wonderful. And he could feel the warmth of her embrace. And her heart—my God, her beating heart—he could feel it beat when she leaned against his chest. No, she was alive, more alive than anyone he had ever known.

When they reached the true "crest" of Plymouth Crest, Alec saw the view of the lake far below the trees, but from an even higher, more majestic overlook. It was stunning. And directly below, about three hundred feet down, sat his home. From this vantage point, he saw the back of his house and all those windows on the first and second floors of his main living room. Beyond this, he could just make out his dirt driveway meandering, under a canopy of trees, onto a single road that winded down the hill. The clouds, now clearing, reflected yellow over the lake. Joy was gazing down at the water too, running her fingers through her long dark hair, just staring. And the sun shone through the clouds, glistening over her pretty face, too.

"Isn't it lovely?"

"Joy, there's something about the way you look."

She turned with a smug smile. "What's the matter with the way I look?"

"I can't put my finger on it," Alec said, "all I know is, I don't think you're being honest with me. Some very weird things are going on, and you're not explaining them."

"Like what? So, what do you think about my idea of the destination being Hawaii instead of St. Louis? Everyone loves a holiday tale in Hawaii more than trains. I once saw a movie about trains. I tell you, it gets pretty damn dreary."

"Why are you so into helping me with my story?"

"I love love songs," she said gazing into his eyes. "I mean…you know, I… I love love stories, and stories are like songs. I'm from L.A., Alec, like you. Just a bohemian who loves the trees as much as you do, and a lover of art, like you. I used to write music. I love love lyrics."

"Like Fifi?"

"What?" she asked. It seemed to snap her out of it. "What do you mean, Fifi? You mean, like, Fifi Graynger, the musician who died in your house?" And she laughed.

"You're beautiful."

"You're not so bad yourself. I thought I heard you say that the other day."

"No, no, you're *too* beautiful, Joy," he said, shaking his head. "I want you to be honest with me. I think you're

Fifi. Fifi Graynger. I don't know how, or why, but you never died, did you? You're Fifi Graynger. That's why you're living near my house, or on the grounds of her house? Or wherever you live. Where do you live, by the way?"

"Are you crazy, Alec? Do I look like that music star? Have you ever seen her?"

No, she didn't look like her. Maybe she'd had plastic surgery? Was that explanation any weirder than the alternative?

Before he could answer, his cellphone rang in his pants pocket. The contact read "Chip."

He raised a finger and walked a couple steps toward the edge of the grassy and muddy cliffside.

"What's up, Chip?"

"Bad news."

"So what's new?"

"Man, it's not that bad. I had my second talk with Reggie, a lot longer this time. He said our famous pop star moved to Plymouth Hill to get away from the Hollywood scene. She wanted to get away from the hustle and bustle, just like someone else I know. She was most definitely the owner. She built the place. She's the one who built your mansion."

"You already said she was the owner."

Alec looked at Joy. Joy just kept smiling, gazing down at the lake.

"Yeah, but here's the bad news. I also researched the tabloids. Alec, Reggie and Joy were *estranged* lovers. They didn't like each other when she passed away."

Alec froze.

"See, they had a huge falling out before Joy died, so I have my doubts, whatever Reggie's saying, that he has legal ownership of the place—unless he's lucky and she set up her will before their falling out. But from what I've researched in magazines and papers, Reggie and Joy were on awful terms when she finally moved into your house."

Alec glared at Joy. Joy didn't turn, but her smile narrowed.

"Are you still there…"

"Why do you keep saying Joy?"

"What?"

"Why are you calling Fifi, Joy?"

"Oh, Fifi was her stage name. Sounds like a stage name, right? But the name she was born with was Josephine. Fifi is a nickname for Josephine. Well, Reggie never referred to her as Fifi when he knew her. On our call, he kept calling her Joy. Apparently, Joy was her private nickname for only her closest friends. See, Joy's a popular nickname for Josephine too."

Alec felt his hand tighten into a fist. His whole body stiffened. Joy still stared at the view, but now she had what looked like a pained expression.

"Here's the good news," Chip continued. "Reggie's planning to visit you and work out all the legal avenues. If he can get legal claim to the deed, we can still do business with him. And why wouldn't he? Apparently, Reggie said that when Joy died, she left no next of kin or close friends. Reggie said he doesn't think there's a will. So who else can lay claim?"

"*Joy?*"

Joy finally turned.

"Joy, Fifi, Josephine, whatever," Chip said. "Does it matter? That lady had a lot of names when she was alive."

"But Reggie said the deceased woman's nickname was Joy? Are you absolutely positive, Chip?"

Joy grunted.

"Sure," Chip said. "So?"

Alec's heart grew heavy. He swooned, feeling dizzy, and the high elevation, which had been a pleasure, sickened him. The facts finally matched his suspicions, but he couldn't believe it. Even now, it looked like he was in the company of his neighbor, someone who had come to his house for a simple morning walk with him. Looking at her, he just couldn't believe the lady beside him was a ghost.

"How…did she…die, Chip?" Alec muttered. Joy grunted again, but he didn't dare look at her this time. "Did Reggie tell you how she passed away?"

"Oh, well, I don't want to tell you that."

"Please, man, tell me."

"If we finally get the deal on your house, you're not going to want to know this."

"How, Chip? I have to know."

"He said she fell from the bedroom balcony to her death. It was suicide. But he fled the country after witnessing it for fear of being accused of murder. There was never anything to implicate him. Ultimately, Reggie claims it was her fans that chased him out of the country. The whole ordeal apparently destroyed his reputation and career. Her fans suspected he killed her, because of their falling out, but it was never proven. I didn't want to tell you about the balcony because that spot is your favorite part of the house."

"He's sure she died?"

With little surprise, Joy looked deadpan now. Guarded. Almost angry. But a single tear fell down her cheek.

"What do you mean?" Chip asked.

"He's positive she died?"

And then, of all people, Joy nodded solemnly. That made Alec feel sicker.

"Alec," Chip replied, "your terrace is like three to four stories high when you account for the grade down the hillside. Anyone falling from your balcony wouldn't do well from that height. He witnessed her fall off the ledge and then he freaked out. He claims it was suicide, but he was so worried he'd be blamed, he ran. Well, he came back. Two days later, Joy's dead body was still lying in the front yard. He called the coroner, but it took the coroner another day to come by—you know how far away you are from everything. But then the body disappeared. So there never was a death certificate. You—damn, this is morbid, Alec—you know, you're in the middle of nowhere. God knows if some animal took her body. Her body was never found so, technically, Josephine Graynger is still missing."

"But Reggie saw her body. You're absolutely positive?"

"Yeah. He's sure. Why?"

"Two days later, he confirmed it? And… Joy is another one of Josephine Graynger's nicknames?"

"Yes. And yes."

Joy grunted yet again, folding her arms.

"Yes," Chip drawled on the phone. "Our pop star died falling from your balcony two decades ago. Why are you acting so surprised? Does it matter? I told you Fifi was the ghost of the house when you purchased it. Look, Alec, don't worry, I can fix all this. Reggie had totally forgotten about your place. He assumed it was taken by the state years ago. If he's telling me the truth, who else can lay claim? He wants to fly over from Costa Rica and see the place. He's saying he'll sell it to us if he can get the deed—unlike his son, who didn't know what the hell he was doing."

Joy shook her head vehemently.

"What?" Alec snapped, glaring at Joy. "What's the matter?"

"What do you mean, what?" asked Chip.

"No, Alec," Joy said in a forced whisper. "No. You can't let Reggie come here."

"Chip, just—"

"No," Joy said again quietly. "Don't let that man come

anywhere near my house. Make sure that asshole stays far away from us. He's a very dangerous man."

"Why?" Alec asked.

"Who are you talking to?" Chip asked.

"I'll talk to you later, Chip."

"Sure. Sure. I'll send you all the details. But here's the best part. Because Reggie had thought the property had been destroyed, he said he's willing to take an even smaller cut than his son for the sale! Isn't that great! I tell you, if bad things keep happening, pretty soon you might have the place for free!"

"Bye, Chip."

"Bye. It's good news, right?"

No. It was some of the worst news Alec had heard in his life.

He shoved the phone back in his pocket. Then the trees and grass surrounding him swayed, and he fought an urge to vomit. He put his head in his hand and closed his eyes tightly.

"Whatever you do, Alec," Joy said, "you have to keep that asshole away from my house. You don't want him anywhere near us. He's a very dangerous man. If you—"

"*Shut up!*" Alec shouted. Joy lurched back. "*Shut up and just be quiet! You're…you're not even real!* Is he right? Are you Fifi's ghost? Of course you are. Where else can you live? You're a ghost. But you seem so real. How? How are you so real? Are you real? Is there anything about you…"

He ran his hand through his short hair. Then he just turned from her and stared at the view. The view, now with clearer skies after the storm, was gorgeous. Gorgeous like Joy. Joy…*his ghost?* For the first time since moving here, he loathed the view. Then he crouched down on his knees, sick.

"Alec, I'm sorry… I really am. I've been watching you for months. I really like you. I wanted to talk to you so many times, and then, when I felt like you liked me, I wanted to touch you. That's why I came to you last night. I watched you for so long, wanting to be with you, because… because…I'm falling in love with you."

"*How can you say that now!*" Then he shouted something completely incomprehensible. "You've been messing with me since we met! Why didn't you tell me from the start what you were?" He gazed down at her bare feet, her perfect feet, without a scrape or a bit of dirt. "No shoes? You never wear shoes, right? But you have flawless feet. That's a weird goddamn ghost thing, isn't it? That's why your feet are perfect, despite rain, thorns, or mud. You're not just Fifi, you're that pop star's ghost."

She nodded.

"Why don't you look like her?"

"I touched stuff up here and there on my face," she said with a shrug. "I thought you'd like me better this way. I suppose it's really no different from putting makeup on. I used to wear a lot of makeup back in the day. I was good at it. I'm good at all sorts of things I put my mind to, Alec. Just like—" She went on and on, but he stopped listening.

"*Why'd you lie to me!*"

"I didn't," she said, shaking her head vehemently. "I didn't lie. I never lied. I was going to tell you everything. I was going to tell everything right now on our walk. I think you were figuring it out. Honestly, it was nice to be around someone who didn't know."

"Did we?" Alec asked, disgusted. "Did last night in my bedroom really happen? Was last night real? I thought that was a dream? Did you seduce me and enter my mind in my dreams? In *your* bedroom, or my bedroom? Or… *Fuck!* Did we…did we make love or not, Joy?" He shook his head and shut his eyes tight. His embarrassment over it made him feel angrier. "How was last night not a lie? You were messing with my mind, hypnotizing me."

"You wanted it too," she said, shaking her head. "All I do is stay around that house all day, watching you. The idea of finally touching you, feeling anyone for that matter, was so... I just wanted to touch you, that's all. Was that so bad?"

"You've been spying on me too?"

"Look. Sorry, I didn't mean to hurt you. That's the last thing I wanted. I think you're a wonderful man. But now I don't care much for your tone."

"Oh, am I losing my temper with *a ghost?*"

"Yes, you are," she said, with eyes wide, nodding. "You sure are. I've learned in my life to avoid people with anger issues. You're sounding like a total dick right now, Alec, just like you did when you shouted at me at the lake when we first met. And the same way you did when you shouted at Reggie's son."

"*Oh my God, was that your son!*"

"*No!*" she shouted, grinding her teeth. "*No! No! Fuck, Alec! No!*"

She turned from him and wrapped her arms around herself, shaking her head. Then her whole body started shaking.

Was she crying? *Was a ghost crying!?*

"Reggie had loads of women, okay, Alec?" she snapped. "I left him! Okay? That's why I came here. You're turning really mean. Reggie was a monster but, really, my relationship with him is none of your fucking business."

Alec just glared.

"You remember being with me last night, don't you?" she snapped, with her back still turned. "What happened between us in your sleep, happened. But it wasn't lust, it was love. I'm frickin' falling in love with you, 'kay? Keeping you asleep was…the only way I could feel you. Touch you. You wanted to touch me back, didn't you? I didn't make love to you because I wanted a fling, damn it, Alec, I made love with you because I'm in love with you! Stop saying, damn it, just stop saying I'm not real! I am real. You see me, don't you? You felt me last night, didn't you?"

"You seduced me. I didn't know you were a ghost. *Fuck…what am I even saying! You're not real now!*"

She turned back. He stepped back in surprise at the sight of the tears now covering her cheeks.

"You have an anger problem! You're shouting at me like a complete dick! It's just like when you threw the kitchen door in my face. For the record, I asked you for consent a million times. I made love to you because I'm falling in love with you. That's all. I don't think I ever really loved a man when I was alive. Being a ghost allows me to… to watch you and I've watched you for months. You're in my house. What else am I supposed to do? I'm not *spying* on you, you're in my house… Look…you're a good man. It wasn't till after I died that I finally found one. God can be cruel. I just wanted to touch you, Alec. Was that so wrong? Sue me!"

She walked around him, hitting his shoulder, and then headed back down their muddy trail.

"Wait! Where are you going?"

Alec ran to her and snatched her hand to turn her toward him, but her fingers felt like fire.

"Fuck, don't ever touch my hands!" she screamed. *"I'm dead! All right! Why did it take you so fucking long to figure that out!"*

"You're a ghost."

"Re-al-ly?" she drawled, her eyes wide. "And you're *de-ns-e.*" She nodded and laughed derisively. "I can't believe it took you this long. Footsteps? Moving furniture? Hovering cups in the cupboards? Well, the house is obviously haunted. Maybe that would have been enough for most people, but not you. How 'bout visions of my naked body popping up from nowhere in your bedroom? Maybe you didn't mind that so much because you desired me too? You needed your incompetent realtor to tell you I was a ghost?

Or that slimeball Reggie? Well, I wouldn't be inviting Reggie to my house. Do you wonder why he left the country? It wasn't over me. I warn you. You want to join me where I am, go invite Reggie here."

"Wait!" Alec snapped, holding his head and shaking it. "Wait a second. Just…quiet for a second! Shit. I can't take all this. Just let me think."

"*Stop thinking!* I told you to stop doing that! That's your problem! It's why you're so miserable!"

"I can't believe this," he finally said. "Just give me time to think."

"You want something to think about? How 'bout you think of this!"

She grabbed his head with both her hands. The force was one surprise—her fingers burning his face was another. Then she lifted his head and kissed him hard on the lips.

It was a strange feeling of pain and desire. The burn was not just physical. His heart had burned to feel her again all morning, still desiring her, more than anything in the world. He had wanted to kiss her. Now it burned.

"I've fallen in love with you, okay, you jerk!" she exclaimed in tears. "But I'll go. Sure. I'll leave. You can only blame yourself. Cause you don't know how to live life, Alec, do you? You worry. That's you. That's why you needed to live in fucking nowhereville. I left because too many people wanted me, you left because you've got too much shit on your mind!"

"Leave me alone for a second so I can think!" Alec cried. "I came here for peace and quiet. There's nothing about you that's quiet!"

"Well, maybe it would be better if I left?" she asked with a devilish grin. "Would you like me to do that? Do you want me to disappear?"

"*Yes!*"

She nodded slowly, glaring at him with tears still falling

from her eyes. But she wasn't sad anymore—she seemed pissed.

"That's not what I felt this morning," Joy said. "Or last night. Who's lying to whom? You don't want to admit your feelings for me, Alec? Fine, no more Joy. Say bye bye. Just don't you be calling me after I leave. Say *bye to Joy, forever!*"

And she disappeared.

And it turned quiet. Very quiet.

Alec heard birds and squirrels rustling the leaves in the nearby trees and felt a light breeze on his face as he was left alone by the overlook. It was as if she had never been there with him. Because…she hadn't. She was a ghost.

The silence almost made him feel worse than her shouting. If there had been any doubt remaining over Joy's identity, it had vanished with the disappearance of her body…unless his sanity had returned and she had always been just a hallucination?

"Fuck you, Alec!" Joy's voice shouted. *"Fuck you! All right? My house is not Reggie's or his son's or even yours! It's mine! Fifi Graynger's! That name once meant something in this awful world! Go away!"*

ALONE ON THE SHORE

THE NEXT DAY, AFTER THE STORM, THE APPEARANCE OF THE hillside of Plymouth Crest had not changed. That same green thrush surrounded all the large tree trunks and brush, but as Alec trudged down the hill, he was forced to keep to the main path to avoid sink holes and puddles under the foliage. Though the sky was clear, he could still smell fresh rain. Only a few wisps of white clouds floated over the lake now. He crossed the main road to the lake. Then he approached his favorite outlook along a natural pier of rocks. He plopped down on a particularly large rock, dropped his bag, and took out his laptop.

He was finishing his book. This was always the frustrating part—being close to being done but not finishing the story.

He typed.

Then he was distracted by the slapping sound of a few geese skidding across water. The wind picked up a bit, and leaves skidded past him. He shivered for a moment as the air blew past his cheeks. He recalled a similar light chill when he first moved here.

Did that herald his ghost?

"Joy?" he asked quietly. "Oh, Joy, I'm sorry. I couldn't believe you were a ghost. You seemed so real."

The wind stilled. Brushing over the water, yellow sunlight flickered. All the while, waves kept quietly lapping over the rocks under him. And he heard an occasional stir of leaves by birds or squirrels in the trees up the road. Otherwise, it was silent. Perfectly still. Lovely…and lonely.

He couldn't type another word.

NOT THAT LOOK OF LOVE

As open as Alec's new home felt, his dining room was queerly small. When Chip introduced the room to him during his last walk-through of the house, it had been almost as an afterthought. A few weeks later, Alec made the room even smaller by adding his large walnut dining table, spanning the entire space. The room was awkwardly and inconveniently located on the opposite side of the house from the kitchen. And it was always dark. The window faced a bunch of trees in his woodsy side yard and, even when it was a bright, sunny day, the room felt shaded.

But tonight, the dining room was special.

Alec lit candles on the white silk tablecloth and poured red wine into two elegant crystal glasses. He straightened his best porcelain plates and silverware. Then he moved a basket full of rolls closer to a yellow and white flower centerpiece. Of course, in Plymouth Hill, there were no fancy restaurants in town. Actually, there wasn't a restaurant in Badger either. But there was Daisie.

After everything was neatly arranged on the table, he sat down on a wooden chair, staring out through the windows, and waited. Leaves rustled due to birds in the trees and a gentle outdoor breeze. The leaves outside were changing from green to yellow and red. It was the sign of fall that everyone raved about in all those pamphlets and state tourist guides.

He gazed down at his left hand, at the golden ring on his wedding finger, over the white linen tablecloth. *Sandra…* It had been over three years since his wife had passed. Her death still weighed so heavily. He remembered her in a formal black dress sitting at the head of the table—her long hair, darker complexion, and wry smile. They watched their little girl. Their daughter Rachel, barely eight years old, sat across from him with hands folded, looking down with eyes closed, saying grace. The little girl was in a white dress and old-fashioned cloche hat. She looked so cute. All the while Sandra sat beside Alec smiling.

That was when Alec remembered catching a stray glance from his wife. That's what he remembered most about that night. Her look: the look of love. That same feeling that he had felt only recently when gazing into...

The doorbell rang.

Daisie had on a long red coat over a lovely flowing charcoal dress and, when he opened the door, whiffs of her perfume smelled like cinnamon. Her long red hair was perfectly straightened, and she wore mascara. But none of that caught his attention as much as the absence of a design on her head.

Alec grabbed the large paper bag from her hands as Daisie hung her red coat on a hanger on a hook on the wall. Then they headed down a hall to their right to the small dining room.

"Hating our cold yet?" she asked.

"No," he said with a chuckle. "I'm loving the fall leaves. The leaves are turning yellow and brown, Daisie. It's wonderful."

"Yeah, suppose we got that. You don't have that much in California, huh?"

"Not like this."

Alec put down the large paper bag on the dining room table and then took out silver trays. Daisie surprised him by throwing her arms around him. It made him uncomfortable.

"This is going to be so much fun!" she cried with a laugh.

"Thanks for coming."

"No, thank *you*, Alec," she said, running her hand through his hair. "This was such a great idea of mine, wasn't it?"

She laughed and removed more white candles and plates from her large paper bag. Opening the trays revealed a large platter of vegetables, mashed potatoes, and a large pre-sliced chicken. Then Daisie sat down at the head of the table. Alec sat beside her, facing the window again. And then…they ate. Quietly. Alec didn't mind the silence. He just watched through the window across from him as the fall leaves stirred in the breeze.

Soon it grew dark. The darkness made their candles feel quaint.

"You still getting haunted by your ghost?" asked Daisie with her mouth full. She swallowed some chicken and then forked a few green beans. Then she touched his hand. "I never got my friend Luminous to come over and exorcise them."

"No," Alec said dismissively. He cut more meat. "This chicken is delicious. Who taught you to cook so well?"

"Mom was a good cook. Did lots of watching."

"The noises stopped about a month ago. I think the ghost got mad or something. She got really pissed at your cards, I think." He chuckled again. "It was right after that when she disappeared."

Daisie laughed and shrugged. But he wasn't entirely joking.

"Well, Halloween's coming. That would be the perfect time for Luminous to come here and run a séance. We can stake out the place and get rid of any ghosts. I'm sure if there's ghosts, he could exorcise them."

"What's Luminous?"

"Luminous is his name, silly. Oh, you should meet him —" She touched Alec's hand and opened her eyes wide. "He's a wizard. Like a *real* wizard, Alec. He's so good at the craft—and powerful. He likes chaos magic and is really amazing at it. He's even better with magic and the occult than I am." She forked some green beans. "How about the house? Did you finally sort out all the problems with the title?"

"Escrow's stuck in limbo," Alec said with a shrug. "The guy who, apparently, might be able to transfer title has to clear a legal mess. Suits me fine. The longer he takes, the longer I can stay for free. No one's living here, and neither the owner nor his son cares about me sticking around until all the legal paperwork is worked out. They just want the money. Problem is that the true owner was a pop star, his estranged lover, Fifi. Fifi Graynger. Also known as Joy."

Alec's red wine glass shook in his hand after saying her name. He had to concentrate to steady it. That was the first time he had mentioned Joy's name out loud to anyone since his mental breakdown...or his haunting... Really, neither madness nor a haunting was comforting.

"*That was that star's name!*" Daisie said, hitting the table. "That was it, Alec! I knew I'd remember it sooner or later. *Fifi. Fifi Graynger.* Yeah, her music was really cool. I copied a couple CDs to cassettes from years back. I should get a CD or stream it, or do whatever people do these days, to listen to her again."

"I'm finally finishing my book," Alec quickly said,

cutting and forking some chicken. "Finally broke out of writer's block, thank God. I don't know what it was about this place, but I couldn't focus. I think it was just too beautiful."

"What are you writing about? A romance, right?"

Alec forked a green bean and then mixed it with some mashed potatoes. When he looked up, Daisie smiled demurely.

"A doctor and a medical sales guy meet in St. Louis on a train."

"Sounds like a joke."

He chuckled and shook his head. "They run from an evil pharmaceutical drug lord who's not only selling tainted pills, but smuggling drugs. Fentanyl and meth."

"And romance, right?" she asked with a wink and a nod. "I love romance. I really do." And she scooted closer.

"Sure."

"I'm happy for you, Alec. I really am. I know it's your dream to write. For some strange reason. I can't stand writing, personally. It's all work to me. I'm perfectly happy running my shop, jibber-jabbering with customers. But you know—" She scooted her chair even closer. Then her smile grew larger. "Well, you know, it gets lonely around Plymouth Hill. With all the snow and all, you can get snowed in. You'll see soon enough. Then not only can you get cabin fever and feel nutty, but you can get lonely." She gazed at the top of his head. She touched his bangs again. "You should…you know, you should let your hair grow out a little more. It'd be nice and wavy that way."

"I don't like my hair," he said as he brushed her fingers away. "I wish it was straighter."

She shrugged. Then she put his wine glass beside hers and reached for his hand.

"Gimme."

He pulled away.

"Come on, Alec. Gimme. Give me your palm. I want to do a reading. I'm not only good at cards, you know. How about a palm reading in your haunted house? I can tell your future. I'm good at divination. Let's try it. It's evening. Nighttime and all these candles bring out lots of magic too."

"I don't believe in all your witchcraft stuff."

"I know you're a nonbeliever. Ever since I met you, I've seen the way you look at the moon on my head."

"Why aren't you wearing it tonight?"

She shrugged. Then she gestured for his hand again. "Gimme. Come on, give me your palm."

He sighed, rolled his eyes, and handed his right hand over.

"Now let's see. Let me see. See this, this is your lifeline, Alec." And she slowly and gently traced his palm with her index finger. "And here is your heartline." And she moved her finger gently on that one too. "And here is your marriage. Hmm."

"What does it say?" Alec asked with a sigh.

"Come on, Alec! You have to believe. Magical intent happens only with belief. If you don't believe, no magic's gonna come of this. So believe and then we can proceed. See…see here, looks like you'll have a long life but lots of bad stuff near the end of it. See how the line gets all broken up. That's common, but yours has many more waves and broken lines than usual. You'll probably develop lots of health problems."

"Oh, great."

"Believe, Alec," she said, rubbing his hand. "Believe."

"I believe already."

She rubbed his palm all over with a chuckle. He doubted stroking his hand was helping with her reading.

"You have very cute hands," she said with a giggle. Then she lifted his palm and kissed it. "Okay, handsome.

Let's not get silly or it will ruin my reading. So, your money line—"

"There's a money line?"

"There sure is."

"You're kidding me. How about a pickup line?"

"Hey!" she said, slapping his shoulder. "What's that supposed to mean? Do you want a reading or not?"

"Not really. I think you just want to hold my hand."

Daisie scowled, feigning anger. But then she leaned forward again with a grimace, rubbing his shoulder and chuckling.

Alec turned to the window and sipped more red wine.

"So you like the food, huh?" Daisie asked.

"Love it."

"Well, I have a confession. I got all of it in Badger. I'm not the greatest cook, Alec."

"Oh, I thought you made it and packaged it."

When he turned back, she was right beside his face. She crept closer, slowly touching her lips to his. And then he felt her hands stroke his hair and rub his back.

"Is this part of the reading?" he asked.

"Sure," she breathed, closing her eyes. "Sure it is, Alec. Aha. Hey"—She playfully hit his shoulder—"stop fooling around."

She grabbed his hand again, laughing.

"Okay, Alec, so you have quite a robust money line, unlike your health line, but, I mean, you were an accountant and you'd have to have money to snatch this place up."

"Just lucked out with a good deal."

"Yeah well, see this line? You can see that there will not be too many challenges with money. Unlike your health."

"Why do you keep talking about my health?"

She shook her head and ran her finger over and over the lines on his palm, stroking his hand more deeply, over and over.

"This, my dear friend, is your heartline. See it? It's got trouble about midway in your life. And here is your marriage line. Hmm…hmm, this is so very interesting. You have two marriage lines, Alec. Two. Not just one. Were you married before you were with your wife that passed away?"

He shook his head.

Then she just sort of stared deeply into his eyes. She reached over and…she was at it again, making out with him over the dining room table. This time, it was not only their lips, but her hands. One of her hands still held his palm, but the other wandered down his leg. She breathed more heavily. And her lips pressed his harder, as he felt her running her hand through his hair again.

Alec jumped as he heard an explosion. It sounded like glass shattering.

"What the hell?" Daisie asked, jumping. "I thought you said the ghost haunting stopped?"

"It did. I thought it had. Haven't heard anything for weeks. Let me"—He stood up—"let me go check. Just stay put, Daisie."

"No, Alec," she groped for his arm. "No. Forget it. You're in Plymouth Hill. There's nobody in your house. Let's get back to our reading."

But he left the dining room and headed across the hallway. He entered the dark living room.

The vision standing by his fireplace didn't surprise him. Half of him was surprised, he supposed, after not seeing her for so long, but the other half had known Joy was "real" all along. Still, had he seen a ghost like this, partly transparent, scowling at him, looking this pissed, when he first moved into this place, he probably would have turned around and run from his haunted house. But there Joy was. Or Fifi's ghost, standing in her usual casual dark blouse and jeans, with arms folded, leaning against the wall by the fireplace, in the darkness, looking furious.

"I don't believe it," he said.

"This is your heartline," Joy mocked scornfully. *"And this is your lifeline. And this is your money line. And this is your 'I'm going to fuck you right now in Fifi's house, Alec,' line."*

"Joy," he snapped in a forced whisper. "Joy… If…" He rubbed his eyes. "If you're really back, just leave us alone tonight. I'm having dinner with my friend."

"The hell you are. That friend is groping you in my goddamn dining room."

"I don't believe this. You're real."

"Yeah. Real. Stop saying I'm not real, Alec! That's pissing me off. I'm a real live ghost that's dead, right here, not in the flesh. Your haunting Joy."

"I kept calling for you," he said in a forced whisper. "I looked every day, all over the house, then down by the lake, calling out your name all over Plymouth Crest and feeling stupid. I kept asking for you everywhere. Why didn't you appear?"

"I needed a break from you. You really got me upset. Anyway, you told me you wanted me to disappear."

"I was in shock."

She turned her back on him and headed into the kitchen as if she were just one of his guests. But then she slammed the door behind her.

"Alec, is everything okay over there?" hollered Daisie.

"Just give me a second."

Alec opened the door to the kitchen.

Joy was leaning against the island with her hands in her pockets. She wasn't transparent anymore. She seemed as real as Daisie. And, unlike her look of rage in the living room, her lips were curled in her smile. Alec tried the kitchen light switch. It didn't work. Joy scrunched her nose and gazed out the kitchen window.

"You want me to disappear?" Joy asked with a shrug. "Fine. But I'm not gonna sit at home like some voyeur watching or listening to you make love to someone else. Watching or listening to people making love is just plain sick."

"Alec?" shouted Daisie. "What's going on over there? You all right?"

"I really can't stand her," Joy said, rolling her eyes.

"Stay there, Daisie," Alec hollered. "I found a rat in the kitchen."

"Oh, cute," Joy said, rolling her eyes. "I'm a rat now."

"Eww, gross," Daisie said. "I hate mice!"

"A rat?" Joy asked, squinting at him. "A rat, Alec?" That made him laugh. Then she laughed too. He hadn't realized how much he had missed that laughter.

"I never said I didn't want to see you," he said in a forced whisper. "I was in total shock, that's all. I kept asking for you. I've missed you, Joy."

"Actually, *disappear* is precisely what you wanted me to do, Alec. You specifically wanted me to *disappear*."

"You asked me if I wanted you to."

"Yeah. And you said *yes!*"

"Fine," Alec said, looking over his shoulder. "Just shush."

She shook her head and heaved a sigh. Then she walked over to the fridge. Raising a middle finger with her back still turned to him, she then, in fact, disappeared again.

"Joy?" he whispered in the darkness. "Joy! Stop it. Come back. Joy?"

"Now you want to see me, weirdo?" asked her voice in the darkness. "After you shouted at me. I like you Alec, and all, but sometimes you can be really weird."

The refrigerator door opened, lighting the room. Then a carton of orange juice floated out and across the floor and hovered over the island. The refrigerator door closed. Then a wooden cabinet door above the kitchen counter opened. A glass floated over to the island. The carton rose by itself and poured juice into the glass.

"Where are you?" he said in a hushed whisper.

"Everywhere. I'm Fifi's ghost. Duh."

"Yeah, but…why are you invisible?"

"You're being dense again, Alec."

"I thought you said you had diabetes."

She just snickered.

The glass was tilted back in thin air, but none of the contents were drunk. "Ah," she said. And then she snickered again.

"I had a lot of fun drinking orange juice with you," he said.

She reappeared and her countenance turned serious. "I enjoyed drinking orange juice with you too, Alec." She nodded. "Yeah, that was fun."

"Alec?" asked Daisie.

"Ohhhh! Get that witch out of my house!"

She slammed the orange juice glass on the island. Then she disappeared once more as Daisie opened the door from the living room.

"Alec?" Daisie asked, opening the door. "What was that? Trying to kill that rat?"

Daisie turned on the light. The light switch worked. Then she walked over to Alec and threw her arms around him, running her hand through his beard.

But she stammered, "Oh my God, babe, you look pale. Why do you look sick?"

"Now she's calling you *babe!*" Joy said. "She's frickin' calling you baby, Alec? Do you know what's next! Ohhh, can she please shut it!"

"*Quiet!*" Alec shouted.

"What?" asked Daisie with a chuckle. "Why?"

"She can't hear me, ditz," Joy said. "I'm only heard

when I want to be heard. There's some perks to being dead."

"Just be quiet, all right?" asked Alec.

Daisie laughed again. "Okay." She ran her hand over his chest. "Okay, sure," she said with a shrug and kissed his cheek. "I'll be quiet, if you want me to be. But I can still touch you. Come on back to the dining room." And she grabbed his elbow. "Come. Let's go back to the dining room, and I'll work more of my magic."

"Course she wants you back there," Joy said, "I warn you, Alec, if you have sex with her, there's gonna be two ghosts in this house."

"You couldn't murder anybody."

"What?" asked Daisie with a laugh. "What's gotten into you, Alec? Why would I want to murder anyone?"

They returned to the dining room. Daisie scooted her chair back to the head of the table and sat down. Then she sipped from her glass of red wine. Alec sat back down and stared out the window at the trees again.

"There really was a rat in the kitchen?" she asked. "Ew, so gross. I guess I shouldn't be so surprised. Your place is really old. You probably should lay traps around the yard. I've got some back at my store I can give you. I set a couple around myself, during autumn, along the foundation of my place. We live in the woods, you know, and it's getting cold enough for them to come inside. Anyway…where were we, handsome?"

"Palm reading."

"Who were you talking to?"

"No one."

"Are you talking to yourself, Alec? That's okay if you are. I do that sometimes. There ain't many people around Plymouth Hill, are there? As long as you're not cracking up from that cabin fever I keep telling you about."

"Maybe I am," Alec said with a chuckle. "I don't know

anymore." He lifted his glass and sipped more red wine. "Sorry. Maybe it is the beginning of cabin fever. Snow or not, yeah, it gets lonely here."

"It sure does."

"*Oh, shut up, Daisie!*" Joy. But it sounded like her voice was hollering from the living room. Daisie nodded slowly. Alec laughed, not at Daisie, but at Joy's rage.

"Now gimme." And she reached out for his palm again. "Gimme your palm. Let's read another line."

"*Another line?*" whispered Joy. "*How about more wine, bitch!*"

Alec lost control of the hand holding his wine glass and splashed its contents in her face.

"*Oh, my god!*" Daisie snapped, jumping up. "*Alec! Alec! What are you doing?*"

"*Daisie!*"

She grabbed her white silk napkin and quickly wiped the wine from her face. Then she blotted her face and clothes.

"*Joy!*" Alec cried, looking up at the ceiling. "*Joy!*"

"Joy?" Daisie asked. "Joy? What the hell is the matter with you! This is hardly joyful. Why do you keep saying 'joy'?"

But then Daisie stopped cleaning her dress and opened her eyes wide. Her lips curled in a large grin.

"*Joy,*" Daisie whispered with a nod. "*Joy.* Wait just one minute. Is that star's ghost here right now, Alec? You called her Joy? You told me that ghost Fifi was also named Joy."

"I did?"

"Joy." Daisie got so excited that she seemed to forget the wine dripping from her hair. "Yes, you did. Joy. That's your ghost's name, isn't it? The ghost's name is Joy."

"Hey, Joy!" Daisie cried, looking up. "Yoo-hoo. Joy! You around here, ghost? Why don't you come and show your-self to me." Then she looked down at Alec. "I'm a witch, remember? These sorts of manifestations come to me. I remember you calling out her name on July Fourth when I was sloshed. I was sober enough to notice, but I thought you were just jibber-jabbering drunk too. I thought it was weird you were talking to yourself, but…you weren't, were you? You were saying *joy*. And Fifi was also called Joy, you said. You're really seeing Fifi's ghost! I can't believe this. You're in contact with the supernatural. This is a haunting and you can actually communicate with her! This is, like, a total class five poltergeist!"

He shook his head. Then he went back to work helping wipe wine off her neck with another white silk napkin.

"I'm sorry, Daisie."

"Forget it. You'd never do this to me on purpose. You're too sweet. That's why I know it wasn't you. Where is she? Where is your ghost, Joy, hiding now? She obviously doesn't care much for me."

"She sure got that right."

Alec stood up. Then his hand was forced again to move without his control. This time, he picked up her red wine glass with a shaky hand and lifted it over her head.

"Alec, what are you doing!" Daisie asked, staring up at the glass.

Too late. The second glass of wine was spilled over her head. Laughter echoed all over the room, and it seemed like this time Daisie heard it too. The laughter circled around the room until finally stopping at the opposite side of the dining room table.

Joy appeared. But this wasn't the ghost Alec had been seeing. It was Joy's face, sort of, but her skin was as pale as the tablecloth. Her eyes were pearly white too, her dress was in tatters, and bloody gashes and cuts covered her arms and chest. Her tattered dress was crimson. One large gash was gaping open under her neck, revealing muscle and sinew. And though her face resembled Joy's, her hair was thin and patchy. But the worst was the bugs. Worms crawled all over her skin, with even a few maggots falling from the thin strands of her hair onto the white tablecloth. Yet all the while, over cracked gray lips, it was Joy's infamous grin.

Daisie screamed.

"Get out of my house!" Joy shouted, jumping up and slamming the table with her palms.

Joy disappeared.

Alec had to grab Daisie before she hit the floor. Then Daisie fought Alec, clamoring out of his embrace.

"I…I have to go," Daisie stammered. "You…you have to go. Oh, my God, Alec, what the hell is in this place? A demon? Get out. Leave this place. Oh my God, I saw her. I actually saw Fifi's ghost! I can't believe it. Alec, I think your house is really haunted. And you…you're talking to…that, that, that thing? Why? And how? You must get out too."

Daisie pulled away from him and clamored to the front door. She grabbed her red coat and hat, threw the door open, and darted outside.

"Daisie!" shouted Alec. "Daisie. Wait!"

In another minute, Alec heard the ignition of Daisie's brown pickup. Then he saw her skid along the dirt road and drive off.

There was laughter behind him. This time it was coming from the living room. He spun around and saw Joy crouched over in the living room, with her head in her hands, bursting into laughter. She was hardly a creature of the night now. As she lifted her head, she had the stunning face she'd always had, wearing her usual informal blouse and pants.

"Bitch. Showed her. Imagine if I looked like that when you first met me. Can you imagine, Alec? You'd already have called a shrink back in July."

"That wasn't funny! How could you do that to her? She probably won't sleep tonight. I should go see her."

"I wouldn't go to her now," Joy said, walking over. She waved her hand, and the front door slammed behind Alec. "Alec, come on. If you show up at her place, she'll freak out thinking I'm with you again. Let things simmer down. Look at how many months it took for you to accept me. Give her time. But"—She put her finger to her chin and looked up in thought—"she'll be back. She's a fake witch and all. She loves ghosts and magic and all this supernatural stuff. Eventually, she'll ask to see me again. Then I think you should just let the cat out of the bag. Let her know about everything, including our time spent together."

"You'll appear for her?" But then he rubbed his eyes. "Wait, I can't believe I'm even talking to you. You're not real."

"Righto. Well, there you go being rude again. You don't believe your eyes? Fine. Sounds like it's time to disappear again. And no, I ain't appearing for Daisie at your whim. I only appear before people I like—or want to scare the shit out of." She chuckled again. "Look, you can date that weirdo, but not in my house. Not in my goddamn dining room, Alec. Geesh. Anyway, I'll go. You want me to disappear, right? Bye."

And she disappeared.

"Wait, Joy! Wait! No, come back."

"You asked for me to disappear," she said in thin air.

"No, I want to see you."

"Nope, I'm still mad. I don't believe you really want to see me."

"I do, Joy."

"Alec, why don't you get out of my house too. Go spend some time with some *real* people. Just keep your lady friends out of my home when you return."

ALONE?

OF COURSE, ALEC COULDN'T SLEEP. HE JUST GAZED UP AT the ceiling in darkness, like he had done so many other nights in this house. It was strange. He loved the house but it seemed to give him constant agitation. Lying on his side, closing his eyes tight, he heard his heart beating fast with his ear lying on top of the pillow. He felt a queer feeling of anguish mixed with excitement. It was a strange mix of feelings.

He sat up. Then he gazed at his bedroom windows. He had drawn the red velvet curtains closed. It was midnight, but moonlight was bright through the crack between the seams of the drapes. He looked outside and trees gently swayed from the breeze under a full moon.

He fell on his back and closed his eyes tight again.

If he was honest with himself, he had liked seeing Joy again…no, he had longed for her. And now, his mind raced with anticipation that, at any moment, she might appear again.

He listened for her. It was so quiet in his bedroom that he felt as if, by straining hard enough, he could hear the sound of his refrigerator downstairs.

The floor creaked. It sounded like footsteps! Someone was in the room.

Before the glass door materialized a woman in a nearly translucent white nightgown. It was the same clothes she had worn on the night of his dream—the night when they had made love. She stared through a gap in the curtains, paying no attention to him, probably gazing down the hill at the lake under the moon. Her profile, the most beautiful he had ever seen, shone in the moonlight. She ran her hand over her long dark hair. He could see her naked body under the thin white nightgown, as perfect and beautiful as her profile.

"Joy?"

She nodded slowly.

"I tried to leave you in peace," she said earnestly, "but I couldn't let you be with her. I just couldn't. Why'd you let that woman come into my home?"

"Did you know Daisie when you were alive?"

She smiled and nodded but still kept her back turned.

"I first saw her when she was a girl. A spunky kid back then too. She visited my home often. I see why you like her, Alec. I've always liked her... I just didn't like seeing her with you. So, you finally accept what I am?"

"Part of me does. The other part thinks I'm crazy."

"You've been tossing in bed all night. Why can't you sleep?"

"If you've been here this past month, why didn't you answer me? I called out so many times."

"I want you to be healthy and happy. Alive. I want the best for you. You should hang out with *real* people, not some *unreal* ghost, as you called me."

"Stop saying you're not real."

"You called me unreal."

Every part of her—her breasts, hips, arms, and legs—and her bare feet (of course)—appeared very real. Only the gown was translucent. And yet, under moonlight, her nakedness felt more natural and innocent than indecent. Though she didn't turn toward him, her grin seemed to reveal that she knew she was being watched.

"Why won't you turn around, Joy?"

"I'm dead, Alec."

"Like my book?"

"Is your book dead, Alec?" she asked with a chuckle, finally cocking her head back. He laughed too. Then their eyes met and, though she was in shadows, he felt as entranced by her eyes as she seemed to be by the view of their lake below.

"Thank you," he said.

"Thanks for what?"

"For letting me stay in your house, Josephine."

"You're the first one I ever let do it," she said with a chuckle. "I scared all the others away."

"Why?"

She shrugged again. "I think you know." Then she went back to staring outside.

He answered by doing something strange. It was the only "normal" strange thing he could think of doing in his haunted house. He turned on his side and closed his eyes.

"Goodnight, Joy. Don't leave me again. I don't want you disappearing."

But as he lay on his side, his heart pounded harder than ever, knowing she was still there.

Then he felt her. Her fingers ran gently through his hair, massaging his head.

"These past few weeks, keeping quiet around you, Alec," she whispered, "have been very hard. I've wanted to talk, to feel you again, for so long."

"I thought your hands were too cold to touch me?"

"Shh... You're finally sleeping. Rest, Alec. Just go to sleep, babe."

EVICTION

Alec felt the same light step in his stride that he had experienced when he first visited Plymouth Crest. He bounded downstairs early in the morning. Then he opened his refrigerator door and laughed as he reached in for his carton of orange juice. He couldn't get his mind off her. When he first got up, just opening the drapes and gazing at the terrace reminded him of when he first saw her down the hill by the lake. Then, walking along his inner balcony, looking down at the living room, reminded him of the time Joy helped Daisie and him up the stairs. It seemed her image shone everywhere in his mind. She haunted him in more ways than with her appearances.

He sat down at his small kitchen table and poured himself a glass of juice, hoping his ghost would join him.

"Joy?"

When she didn't answer, he opened the laptop on the kitchen table.

No wonder she liked stories. She was Fifi the music star. She had been in movies and the entertainment industry. But where had she gone now? Where did she ever go when he didn't see her? If she was a ghost, wasn't she always in the house?

Thankfully, the keys on his computer moved under his fingertips. He wrote a full chapter in an hour. It was action-packed, with the police chasing his main character, the doctor. The doctor had acquired evidence that the medicine was tainted and was planning on releasing it to the authorities—only the police were in on it too. Some of the cops had turned bad and were part of the conspiracy. So now the doctor was searching for her lover downtown, to warn him.

After editing for several hours, and realizing he'd have to add yet another chapter or two to finish his novel, he heard the front doorbell ring.

He gazed through the glass kitchen door—it was very foggy outside.

The doorbell rang again.

Could it be Joy? But why would she ring the doorbell?

He ran excitedly to the front door. Looking through the peephole, he saw that Joy wasn't there. Three gruff men stood on his front porch. Two had the countenance of security guards. One reminded him more of a pimp—a tall, pale-skinned man with a mustache, wearing a violet suit and green driver cap. The other two burly men, one bald and the other with a buzz cut, wore sunglasses, black T-shirts, and pants.

Alec looked down at his robe and pajamas, shaking his head. "Who is it?"

"Name's Reginald Tealman," said the tall one in violet. "These are my friends, Oscar and Terry. Mind opening up so we can talk about the house?"

"My realtor didn't tell me you were coming today. Did you finally sort out the title?"

"Yes. And we came all the way here to go over it with

you. How about you open up and we can talk. It was a very long trip, amigo."

Alec unlocked the chain and opened the door.

The three of them took off their coats and hung them on hooks by the door. Then the two giant men walked around him and did what everyone always did first upon seeing the house. They headed into the living room and stared up at the mezzanine. Reginald just looked around the foyer admiring the view.

"Reggie," he said, giving Alec his hand to shake. "I haven't been here in such a long time. Such a long time. I had been told the house burned down. Hearing it wasn't gone… I still figured it'd be all boarded up and in disrepair. No, no, this is incredible. It looks exactly the same as when Joy lived here twenty years ago. Except her furniture's gone."

"Your son sold or gave most of it away. Didn't he tell you?"

"No."

"I should get dressed," he said with a nod. "Why don't you guys stay downstairs, and I'll be back in just a minute. I can brew you three some coffee?"

"No need. This will only take a moment."

"Wow!" exclaimed one of the burly men—the bald one. "Wow, boss! This house is so good!"

"Told you," Reggie said with a laugh.

"But in the middle of the woods," said the guy with the crew cut, laughing and looking up too.

"Joy sure knew how to live," Reggie said, walking into the living room and staring at the upstairs balcony with them. "She made herself a castle in the forest. Only she would do that." Reggie shook his head and then addressed Alec. "You'll need to do more than get dressed, sir. You'll be needing to grab *all* your clothes. This mansion was never sold to you because it never belonged to my son. It belongs to me. Joy and me." Then he turned and smirked. "I'd like you to leave."

"Excuse me?"

"No one should ever have pretended to sell this place to you. After I receive title, trust me, you won't be able to afford it. I think I might stay for the winter." He walked to the living room window, gazing upstairs and shaking his head. "Wow, it's not only in good condition, it's in wonderful condition. You sure kept up the place."

"Do you have the deed to prove ownership?"

"Get out," Reggie said, losing his smile. He cocked his head back and glanced at Alec. "Why don't you get out now."

"Go," Joy said in a forced whisper. "Go!" It sounded like she was upstairs. "Get out, Alec! Reggie means it."

"What are you talking about!" Alec cried. "I already paid the deposit and moved all my stuff in."

"*Stop it, Alec!*" warned Joy in a forced whisper. "*He's dangerous!*"

Alec turned to his right toward the sound of her voice. Joy materialized in her blouse and jeans in the hallway, shaking her head vehemently. Her eyes were wide open with an expression he had never seen before. She looked afraid.

"Terry, go get my bags from the car, will you?" Reggie asked, feigning a grin. "We're moving in." Then he turned to Alec again with a fake smile. "You're moving out."

"The hell I am!"

"The offer given to you by my relation," Reggie said, "a boy who never owned this house, was not only inappropriate, it was ridiculous. Unless you intend to hand me ten times the said amount, title of this house will not be handed to you, sir. I might be willing to sell the place at a higher price... But...well, looking at it"—Reggie looked around him, shaking his head—"it seems my wife didn't just build herself a mansion, she built a little resort. A vacation home. People might come to the mountains for skiing, eh? Well, skiing was the lie that bitch told me to bring me here. With the place in such pristine condition, we could flatten more of the trees and make some slopes. Or, at the very least, make it into a place to stay for hunting. Joy ran a frivolous, wasted life, but she sure had an eye for fashion and architecture." He walked to the living room windows and stared outside again. Then he tapped the glass with his index finger. "I really had thought this place was gone," he said again, more to himself. "Oh, Joy."

He plopped down on Alec's black leather sofa. His goons were still staring at the mezzanine above them.

Reggie took out a cigarette and lighter from his pocket and lit it. Alec didn't have any ashtrays.

"The place will naturally fall to me, sir," he said, taking a deep drag and leaning back. "You certainly don't own my wife's house. You must get out now."

"Joy was never your wife!"

"*Shut up, Alec!*" Joy said between her teeth. "*Shut up and forget it! Stop being dumb and look. His guards are carrying guns.*"

Alec looked toward their large chests and protruding stomachs. Indeed, she was right, both guards were carrying sidearms.

"*Get out while you* can," Joy said. "*He means what he says. He will hurt you if you don't go. We can think of something later.*"

She appeared in the foyer. But she was translucent, and he could see right through her to the front door.

"Did he hurt you?" Alec asked.

Joy opened her eyes wide, vehemently shaking her head and putting a finger over her lips.

Then she completely disappeared.

"Is this guy loco, boss?" Terry asked with a laugh. "Maybe living out in the woods too long? Who in the hell is he talking to?"

"I get this is sudden," Reggie said with a smirk, standing up. Then he walked right up to Alec and got in his face. "But the house simply isn't yours. I can't have you stay. If you stay, you could be considered a squatter. Then you could go to the police and do what squatters do. Squat. I can't have you do that. In this state, you'd have rights to my house. Don't worry. I'll arrange for all your stuff to be sent back to you—all your chairs, tables, furniture, or whatever. I'll send you back your stuff. Just leave me an address. I just need your body to get the fuck off my premises now. Understand? And don't plan on coming back. My friends and I will be staying here for quite a while until all the paperwork clears with my attorneys."

"Then *you'll be* the squatter!"

"*Quiet, Alec!*" warned Joy again. "*Don't argue with him!*"

But somehow Joy's fear angered Alec even more. He glared at Reggie, ready to deck him. But, in his periphery, Alec watched Reggie's goons moving to stand behind him. Their hands lay over their gun holsters.

"I'm the owner, you motherfucker," Reggie said calmly, blowing smoke from his cigarette into his eyes. "Get dressed, grab your shit, and get the fuck out. *Now.* Or my two friends will help you out."

THE POLICE REPORT

ALEC LEANED FORWARD, IN A WOODEN CHAIR AT A DESK, IN a large room filling out forms. There were two large desks, though the one beside him was unoccupied. Three empty chairs were next to the main entrance near sliding glass doors. And to his left was a very small area sectioned off by blue-painted bars. Inside this cell were a sink and a cot. He had always thought jail cells at police stations were only in the movies. Sitting across from him at the desk in a tan police uniform, un-shelling peanuts and scratching his gray hair, was, of course, Sheriff Denson—probably the only police officer in the county. Peanut shells were all over his desk. Above him, "Badger Police Department" was painted in blue.

"I'm really sorry this happened, Alec," Denson said. "Daisie's told me how nice a person you are. I mean, really, we all appreciate you in our town. July Fourth was sure a lot of fun."

"All my stuff is in that house," Alec said, absent-mindedly penciling in more squares on the forms.

Denson offered him some peanuts from his bag. Alec shook his head.

"You know, I can't just throw him out," Denson said frowning. "The law protects people inside a property without a warrant."

"That's what he said. He forced me out so I wouldn't be the one claiming the property. He came in with guns to do precisely what he accused me of doing. He forcefully had me leave."

"But if I don't have the right documentation—"

"I know, Sheriff. I know. You told me all this already."

"Look, these crazy city-dwellers—unlike you, Alec—don't care much for our small town. Stay put until the snow comes. You'll see. The minute he's snowed in for a few weeks, he'll come running from your property. You'll see."

"The fool wants to rent the place out for skiers."

"*Skiers!*" Denson said, bursting into laughter. "Skiers? No one's gonna vacation at Plymouth Crest for skis and a creemee! Here? Never." Denson tried his best to stop laughing. "Ridiculous. We get hunters, but never skiers. That's why your house was abandoned for so long. The mansion's wonderful and all, but it ain't gonna draw tourists. There's not much here but a lot of snow and an iced-over lake with pretty fall trees. That's all and we love it. But just you wait for the mud season. If the ice doesn't get those strangers out, the mud will make 'em run away. You'll see. No, I figure only writers like yourself would be interested in living in that place."

"Then I should get it."

"I know, Alec. I know. Look, Daisie's sure fond of you. I knew her parents, you know. She told me how much she likes talking to you. I tell you, if there's anything I can do to get your house back, I will. I'll head on over the minute I have the necessary paperwork. But knowing the way bad people work—and I've been sheriff for thirty years, Alec, thirty years, mind you—bad people are impatient. Don't play their game. Don't you be impatient too. I advise you to just wait this out. Just talk to your lawyer folks back home, and we'll work everything out. Look, you've got the whole town on your side."

"Sure," Alec said with a sigh, turning the page over.

Denson threw more nuts in his mouth. Then he added, "I bet the minute he gets trapped in ice, he'll be itching to leave. Just give him a couple of weeks. Don't worry. I see them run all the time."

Alec nodded again, signing the bottom of the page.

"I sent one of them books of yours over to my niece, Emily. *Fear of the Spark*. An interesting book, Alec. I think she's liking it a whole bunch."

"Was it a paperback?" he asked, turning the next form over. There were more blank lines to fill out. He detested forms. He had spent years dealing with them and wanted nothing to do with it anymore. "Or hardback? Or an ebook?"

"Not sure. I can ask her."

"I can sign it if it's a book, Denson," he said with a nod. "Just let me know."

"That'd be really kind of you. You sure are a decent guy, Alec. I tell you, you have to be one of the nicest men I've ever known."

Alec looked up and forced a smile. He knew the old man was doing the best he could.

"Well, I got some police business to attend to." And he stood up. "When you complete all those forms, just leave it here on my desk and I'll sort it out. If you need anything else, anything at all, just come by the station and I'll see what I can do to help you."

When the sheriff left, Alec filled in his address. Again. The address of the house that was apparently no longer his. Then he reached into his pocket and took out his cellphone. His best friend had sent about a gazillion texts after

Alec texted that he had ignored. He hadn't been ready to talk to his friend until now.

"Alec!" Chip hollered, answering the phone. "Alec, what the hell happened? That motherfucker threw you out of your own house!"

"Yeah. Looks like there'll be no commission for you."

"Shut up, man! I don't give a shit about my commission! You said he came in with guns. Was that a joke? Did he point a gun at you?"

"No, but his friends were armed and looked like bouncers from a club."

"I can't believe this."

"Forget it. If he's right and he's the closest kin to Joy, legally, he'll have the greatest chance of getting the house, whether he's an asshole or not."

"I'll talk to the kid again."

"I kinda doubt Reggie ever talks to his son. Anyway, he'll be able to claim the house before Robin can."

"Well, I can now tell you emphatically that Reggie never got married to Fifi. I haven't seen a marriage license or heard anything about that in all my research. Nor was it ever mentioned by her or fans in her magazine interviews, and I'm sure it would have been. I'm thinking we could have better luck if I can find Fifi's relations. Fifi's family might have better luck getting rights to the place." Chip heaved a sigh. "No direct relatives are known, but I don't know, maybe a cousin or uncle or…something. All this… sounds like now it's becoming dangerous. What a fucking mess. The greatest mystery is the signatures. I'm having a rough enough time just trying to figure out how the hell the property tax and insurance have been signed off in that pop star's name. Maybe if we can discover that mystery—"

"I think I know why."

"Why?"

"Forget it, Chip."

But his friend didn't stop yapping. Alec stopped listening. He jumped up, running his hand through his hair. He gazed through the sliding glass door at "downtown" Badger. From here, he could see the town square, old brick buildings surrounding their main street. About a block down was a gas station, hotel, and Walmart. That was the entire town. A few people in long coats walked along the sidewalk. It would be snowing soon. For Badger, this was the busiest thoroughfare in a hundred miles.

"Chip, it's not your fault this time," Alec finally said, heaving another sigh. "Just, don't worry."

"Actually the whole damn thing is my fault."

"I found the listing."

"I'm so sorry I called that jerk. That mistake is on me. I'll get it fixed."

"Forget it, I say."

That's when Alec spotted a woman in a black shawl passing the glass door. He'd recognize that face anywhere. *It was Joy!* He ran to the exit, but the glass doors couldn't open fast enough.

And the minute he stood outside, she vanished.

"Joy! Joy! Stop disappearing so I can talk to you!"

"Huh?" asked Chip on the phone. "What the hell are you talking about?"

"Forget it, Chip. Forget it. Yeah, everything's shit, but I don't blame you. It's all right. I'll figure something out."

"Hang in there," his friend said, sounding miserable.

Alec ran down the sidewalk, chasing his vanished specter in the direction from which she had disappeared. But by the time he reached the end of the square, he stopped running. Because she was gone.

GHOST MAKEUP

Alec ran his fingers through his hair, leaning over the white leather couch in Daisie's house. Across from him were two matching chairs and a small table. To his left, Daisie's kitchen was small enough to fit a mobile kitchen in a trailer. Daisie's home was just this room, the kitchen, and a bedroom and bathroom near the supply room in the back of her store. But everything was well maintained. The white couch didn't have a blemish on it. There were many plants and flowers, and a pleasant tea and ginger smell permeated her quarters. She had told him she was a green witch, whatever that meant.

"It's not Plymouth Crest," Daisie said, handing Alec a pillow, "but it's home. The couch folds out into a bed and, being that Plymouth Hill is in the middle of absolutely nowhere, you won't be waking up from too much noise." She chuckled. "Except coyotes. And there's an occasional idiot racing down the road honking his horn. You know, my place is by the main road."

It was approaching noon, but the only small window in her home, in the kitchen, admitted little light. The white mist was still thick.

Daisie wore no fancy makeup or moons on her forehead. Alec had surprised her so much that she was still wearing her morning robe.

"Anything," Alec said, shaking his head. "I mean, everything, everything is great, Daisie. Just, thank you so much for having me here at your place. I'm sorry I barged in."

"Are you crazy?" she asked, sitting in a white chair across from him. "That fucking asshole had no right to throw you out of your house, Alec. I'd rather sock the creep in the nose."

"You heard what Sheriff Denson said."

"He's just scared of lawyers."

"I probably won't be here much longer to bother you."

"Where're you gonna go, kiddo?"

"Don't know," he said with a sigh. "I'll probably just need a place for the night. I can stay in the hotel in Badger tomorrow."

"Stay the whole week. I don't mind your company, Alec. You come by the shop every day to talk anyway."

"Thanks so much, Daisie. You're a really good friend."

She leaned over and gave him a squeeze.

"These last few months with you have been wonderful," she said. "I really love it when you come by. You've taken away some of Plymouth Hill's dreariness."

He nodded.

Then he stood up and approached the small window in the kitchen. It faced Daisie's "backyard" behind the store. There were maple trees and bushes out there, but this morning all he could see was a thick white wall of fog. Perfect for hiding things. Things like...

Ghosts? Joy must be out there, somewhere. Wherever did she go when she disappeared?

"You're a good friend," Alec muttered again. "I appreciate it but—"

"They really had guns?"

Alec nodded.

"And your ghost told you to run?"

"She was scared. That was so weird. I've never seen Joy scared of anything before."

"I find it hard to imagine that ghoul being afraid of anything."

"That's not the way Joy looks," he said with a chuckle. "She was just trying to scare you. Or at least it's not how she looks to me."

"How does she look to you?"

Alec shook his head and finally tore himself from her window.

"Daisie, I'm gonna wander a bit outside—step out for some fresh air. I'll be back in half an hour."

"Kinda dreary out there. This wet weather, you know, is a bit of a prelude before our real fun in Plymouth Hill: rain, sleet and snow."

"I'll be right back," he said with a chuckle.

He rubbed her shoulder on his way out and opened her door to the store. The Corner Store was the only way to leave her place.

But when he reached the exit, Daisie hollered, "Going to see her?"

Alec turned. Daisie was standing with her arms folded, leaning against the doorway to her home.

"Going to see your ghost?" she repeated sternly. "You can't walk far in that thick fog, Alec. I'm guessing you're going to try to find your new love interest."

"What do you mean?"

"I heard the way you speak to her. I saw it the night of our dinner when she was a ghoul—or before she appeared as a ghoul—and I remembered it on the Fourth. I've had my share of men, Alec. I'm no spring chicken, you know— just never really wanted to be tied down. That's my problem, I suppose. I never settle with anyone, except Plymouth Hill. But I know when a man cares about a lady. You are way beyond palsy-walsy when you talk to her."

"She's just a ghost."

"I know that. But do you?"

"What do you mean?"

"Look, I'm your good friend," she said raising her hand. "I don't want you to get hurt. Just because you don't believe in ghosts, doesn't mean they don't exist. Fifi's ghost has been haunting you. That's a fact. But, unlike our friendship, and after everything you've told me, this ghost seems to really like you. She seems far beyond the friend zone." She raised her hand again. "That's okay, Alec. Truly, I only mention this because I care about you. You're my good friend and that's all that counts. But I'm worried about you. You can't be in love with a ghost, Alec. You can't fall in love with someone who's passed away."

"Daisie," he snapped, "with all that's happening right now, are we going to talk about this now?"

She looked down. Then she shook her head. "Sorry… I just don't know when else will be a good time. Forget I said anything."

"I'd love it if you met her. Not the monster she showed you. Joy. Joy's wonderful. She's so happy and full of energy. She's kind and so caring. Just…thanks for letting me stay the night at your place. Thanks so much. I'll be in the hotel in Badger by tomorrow."

"The hell you will," she hollered as he opened the door outside. "You're staying until you get your house back, Alec."

"Okay. I'll be right back, Daisie."

Walking outside, he could not believe how thick the white fog had become. He couldn't walk much farther than five feet without nearly bumping his head into a tree. He couldn't remember Plymouth Hill ever being this foggy. But the weather fit his mood.

Of course, Daisie was right. He was looking for Joy. And, if he was being honest with himself, it wasn't just to talk to her about their problems. They had finally made up last night. He was so looking forward to spending time with her again. But now this had happened.

Not only did he want the house back—he wanted Joy. And he thought maybe if he was alone again she'd come to him.

Pretty soon, every tree trunk started looking the same in the white fog. He actually worried he might get lost. He tried to keep in a straight line from Daisie's house, and as he gazed back, he could barely make out the dim yellow light from her home.

"Joy?" he said among the white wisps of smoke. "I saw you in Badger. And then I saw you around Reggie. I know you're here. Somewhere. Just show yourself. Please. Come on. Where are you? Joy? Joy?"

"Seems there's not much joy around here now, Alec," Joy said, sounding morose as hell. He barely recognized her voice, as she had never sounded so down.

"Where are you?"

"Here."

She materialized before him in the thick white mist, wearing her usual blouse and jeans, only a couple paces from him. She was leaning on a tree trunk. She put out her arms and they embraced. Then she shook in his arms. Was she crying? He gently tilted up her chin. Sunlight shone through the fog, illuminating her eyes and cheeks. Her face seemed to glow in the mist as tears streamed from her eyes, despite her attempts at a smile.

"First he ruins me, now you." Though tears fell, her voice was crisp, almost angry. "I wanted you to have my house. I really did. Even if we never spoke again after our first fight, I always wanted my place to be yours. I think you're wonderful."

"Did he hurt you?"

"What?" she asked, wiping her eyes. "Why ask about me? I thought you were looking for my help?"

"Why do you seem afraid of him? Was he your murderer?"

"Yes."

She moved a few paces into the fog, almost disappearing. Alec reached for her hand, but she quickly snatched her fingers away.

"Damn it, Alec, don't touch my hand! Why don't you get that I died?"

Somehow shouting at him seemed to make her more upset than ever. She fell on her knees, covered her head, and wept.

"Oh, Joy," he said, rubbing her back. "Joy… I'm so sorry."

She lifted her hand, batting him away. He just stood over her.

"It's okay," he said, "if you…cry."

"It isn't." She shook her head. "What good does crying ever do? Anyway, you came for my help."

"I'm sorry, Joy."

"My name's not Joy."

She slowly forced herself up. Then she straightened and turned very serious.

"I'm Josephine. I loved the stage name Jewel, but it was already taken. Reggie loved Fifi. I think he picked Fifi because it sounded immature and easy to push around. Like, your fluffy feathery Fifi. Well, she became quite well-known, didn't she? The world knew me as the funny-go-lucky Fifi. I hated it. You called me unreal? Back in L.A., Alec, I was more unreal alive than dead. Even Fifi's appearance was made up. Well, not for you, Alec. I don't want to deceive you of all people. You don't deserve deception. Let me show her to you."

Her face blurred amidst the thick white smoke. At first, he felt as if the mist were simply thicker, but then he realized it was Joy's magic.

Joy transformed. She had the same face, but different. Her nose was hooked. Her eyes narrower. Her skin less vibrant and smooth. There were blemishes on her forehead. And her hair was dusty blond, not black. She was imperfect. Her makeup was thicker, she had hair in a ponytail, and she wore a T-shirt with baggy pants. This was like the picture of that rock star he had googled.

"This is Josephine when she was a star. This is how the world remembered Josephine Graynger: as Fifi. And this is what that asshole Reggie, my agent, created when he launched her career. I made up my appearance as Joy for you, just as Reggie made up Fifi.

"When I lived, Alec, I wasn't a singer, I was a goddess. But I was *Reggie's* goddess. Because"—Her voice finally broke again—"Shit…" She turned from him. "Joy might have been a fuckin' great singer, yeah, but inside Joy was never *joyful*. That was Reggie's worst joke."

Alec gently turned her toward him. She smiled woefully.

"No joy, Alec," she said, shaking her head. "No joy. Reggie came up with Joy as a pet name. But the thief could never give joy to anyone but himself. He might have given me stardom, but, yeah, he hurt me. He hurt me a lot. He even beat me. But his abuse was nothing compared with his blackmail. After creating Fifi the rock star, he pushed me around with money and drugs, told me who to hang around with and what to do with my time. I think it was when he finally proposed changing my stage name to our private name, Joy, that I mustered the courage to give him the middle finger.

"That's when I built our mansion on Plymouth Crest. Because Fifi wasn't as dumb as the world thought. I read every contract. I knew how to make my money. So many in the music world don't get that. And I think Reggie despised that I did.

"With my money I built our castle in the clouds. I worked with a contractor and built my princess palace with all the money I had made—not only to get away from Reggie, but to leave California, my fans, and the whole goddamn fake world. And I did. I ran and found peace here—until that motherfucker managed to come and rip that away too."

She shook her head vehemently, and her eyes opened wide.

"He took everything from me, Alec! Everything! He might have taken your house, but he tore up my dream! When I finally found real happiness, he killed me! I had only lived in the house for two weeks. Two goddamn weeks, Alec! That was it! Just two weeks before I died!"

Alec touched her back, but she shook him off. She raised her hand and turned from him.

"But you know," she muttered quietly, looking down. Then she even smiled. "When that dick finally managed to kill me, it wasn't so bad. Death freed me too. You know how much I love it here. Maybe that's why God made me haunt Plymouth Crest. Only when I died was I really able to enjoy it. Oh, I love it here so much." She smiled woefully at him. "And then I was lucky enough to meet you."

She reached for him and they embraced again. Then she reached up and kissed his cheek and lips. Their eyes locked in the white fog and, though it was Fifi's face, it was Joy's eyes.

"Then you came," she said with a nod. "After years of searching. So...what do you think of my depressing life story?"

"I only wish I could fix it for you."

"I know." She laughed, leaning her head against his chest. "You're such an amazing man. I had to die to finally meet one."

"Fifi's face is beautiful."

"Really?" She laughed. "You think so? I thought Joy would be so much prettier for you."

Alec shrugged.

That's when her face altered back to Joy. In a flash, her skin turned silky smooth, her nose straightened, but those eyes remained the same.

"But I love the way you look at me when I'm Joy. I've loved it ever since I broke into my kitchen. But, Alec, I heard what Daisie said to you. She's right. I *am* a ghost. Josephine died. You should be with someone real, like her, not someone who passed away."

She leaned her head gently against his chest, and they stood there, in an embrace, for a long while as the mist slowly cleared. And it was wonderful.

Quickly, perhaps magically, the mist cleared, and they were surrounded by the familiar trees and thrush with only wisps of leftover white fog. Sunrays shimmered between the yellow and red leaves as wisps of white smoke brushed over his ghost.

"Why were you looking for me?" she asked, letting go of him. "How can I help you? After seeing that creep, I guess I needed to dish out all my shit on someone. Thanks for that. But how can I help *you*, Alec?"

"I want your house back."

"You can't fight him," she said, shaking her head. "If Reggie came for the house, he already figured out a way to take it. He's a horrible man. Why do you think he left the country? It wasn't just me. It was probably over a bunch of his other crimes. His pen and paper are his worst weapon. He's an attorney. Those goons with him didn't come to shoot you, they came to drag you out the door with their meathead arms. The guns were just theater."

"What if you were to haunt him?"

"I don't think he'd scare."

"You might be able to frighten him. Or, at the very least, maybe grab their weapons and—"

"Alec, I said he brought those guns to intimidate you, but that doesn't mean he won't use them if he has to."

"I need to get your house back."

"Why is my house so important to you?"

"Not for me. For you. Don't you see, Joy? If I lose the house, I leave, but if you lose it, you're stuck here. If he keeps the house, he'll trap you all over again, this time not in L.A., but in Plymouth Crest as a ghost. I know you're the one who's maintained the upkeep of the place. Not just cleaning throw-up on the stairs, or dusting a stair rail, you've taken care of everything, Joy, for years. You love that house. So, why would you want to give it to a guy who murdered you?"

"*I don't, Alec!*"

"We both want him gone," Alec said with a nod. "Let's make him go."

"It's always been this way with him," she said with a nod. "He's stolen everything from me. He even stole credit for most of my songs. But he'll take more than your house from you if you confront him. He'll take your life. Just… just go on with your life without me. It's not safe. You need to leave."

"If you want me to go, I'll go," he said. "After we get your house back. It's not just for me, I want to help you now. You said he took everything. Don't let him take your house."

"Hmm," she said, cocking her head back, "I thought you were searching for my help?"

"Haunt him, Joy."

"I can…try. For you, Alec. I will."
"No. For us."

They returned together to Daisie's Corner Store. By the screen door, he caught Daisie doing her usual—leaning on the counter in front of her and thumbing through her cellphone. But just as Alec opened the door and the bells jangled, Joy vanished.

"Alec?" asked Daisie. "Did you find her? The fog's finally lifting."

"Joy, please show yourself," he said, searching behind him. "Joy, please?"

She appeared on the threshold beside him. She wasn't a creepy ghoul from a cemetery or a pop star. It was his ghost, Joy. And, as usual, she looked vivid, as if Alec had found a woman straying in the forest.

Daisie lurched back in surprise with her eyes widening.

"Hi," Joy said with a wave.

"I'm…Daisie," Daisie said, forcing a smile.

"I'm Josephine's ghost. I've known you all your life, Daisie."

GOOD OLE HAUNTING

Alec and Daisie were lying on their stomachs on the cliffside, in thick snow coats, staring down at the house that had been stolen from him. Joy was on her stomach too, leaning her chin on her hands, wearing her blouse and jeans, barefoot. Alec and Daisie gazed through binoculars. The eye pieces were like her flashlight. They were military grade equipment and Alec could see, literally, a dime on his coffee table in the living room. It was bright down there. The lights in the house lit up the whole valley.

None of Reggie's goons were asleep yet. One of them was throwing sheets on the couch. The other was tossing a pillow on the floor. He couldn't spot Reggie. No…he could just make out the dick in a robe walking along the inner balcony, smoking another cigarette without an ash tray.

"What are you wearing?" Daisie cried.

Alec laughed. Joy had changed her clothes. She was wearing green army fatigues.

"It's a military strike, right?" Joy asked with a wink. "Figured I'd dress the part. I can change into blue SWAT gear if you prefer?"

"I can't believe I'm in the company of a ghost," Daisie said, rolling her eyes.

"Can't believe I'm hanging with a witch," Joy rebuked.

"Well, if you didn't know, witches don't like ghosts," Daisie said.

"That's not true. What about Wendy and Casper?"

"Was Wendy a witch?" Daisie asked, furrowing her brow. "I thought she was just a cute little girl in a red hoodie?"

"Can you wear your normal clothes, Joy?" Alec asked.

In a flash, Joy was back to wearing her blouse and jeans without shoes.

"Just trying to get us in the mood. But I don't think you want me to wear *normal* clothes, Alec. That'd probably be a white sheet. You know, like a funeral shroud."

"What's the plan, Alec?" Daisie repeated. "Why are we waiting till they fall asleep?"

"Joy's the plan," Alec said with a chuckle. "That asshole doesn't know we have his girlfriend's ghost. Joy's going to do some good ole haunting."

"Will you appear as a dead ghoul again?" Daisie asked. "That was really good. It totally freaked me out."

"The direct approach doesn't work as well as you might think," Joy said, shaking her head. "I find going all out gets the creepy supernatural lovers, like you, only more excited. You'd be surprised what actually scares people out of a house. It's small things: opening a door, turning off lights, running the faucet, footsteps. I've been haunting for years. Trust me, I know."

"I remember you doing that when we first met," Alec said.

"Kept you up at night, didn't I?" Joy said with a wink. "I'm good at what I do. I've always been good at everything I do, including haunting unwanted guests. Course, you were never unwanted, Alec."

"Do your best against him," Alec replied with a nod.

Then he looked down at his house through the binoculars again.

"What are you and I going to do, Alec?" Daisie asked.

"After you scare them, Joy, disarm them. Take their guns. Then, if they all go running from the house, Daisie, you and I will go inside and call for the sheriff."

"Sheriff Denson won't do shit," Daisie remarked.

"For sure," Joy said.

"But that's all he has to do," Alec said. "Nothing. If we disarm them and they vacate, we can take back the house. Then Reggie will have to throw me out again to reclaim it. We'll at least have the law on our side, for now."

"Reggie's too smart," Joy said, squinting and shaking her head. "A few doors opening is not going to scare that jerk. We have to do something big. He already heard the place is haunted. My usual tricks aren't going to work. And even if we manage to make them all run, what's gonna stop him from coming back?"

"You have to try, Joy," Alec said.

"Let's get your house back, Alec," Daisie said. Then she glanced at Joy. "Your house, Fifi."

Joy nodded.

Then Daisie took a compact from her pocket. She used the flashlight in her cellphone to check herself in the mirror. She took out a pencil and started darkening the edges of the quarter moon on her forehead.

"What are you doing?" Joy asked, amused.

"Re-drawing my moon. It brings down kundalini from Hecate above in the sky down to my center. It will help us fight."

"Well, I suppose, if you get to wear your moon on your head, I should get to wear my army fatigues. Right, Alec? You know my cousin Judy was a sergeant in the army for real. And I played a sea captain in high school. Or was it a pirate? Hmm, can't recall. But seems to me if we're gonna be creeping inside a house, I should look the part and be totally ready for a fight too."

And when Alec looked at her again, she had already changed back to her green army uniform. Alec laughed again.

"What planet is she from?" asked Daisie.

"Los Angeles," Joy said. "Same place as Alec."

"Okay, Joy!" Alec gestured to the house after the lights shut off. "Go! It's time. Do your worst... or, your best. Just scare the shit out of him."

For a while, it was just dark and quiet. Literally, all Alec heard were the shuffling of his and Daisie's bodies in the leaves and the crickets.

But then he saw lights flash in the living room. The brightness was jarring. It startled the men lying on the floor too. One of them jumped up and ran to the light switch, but the lights shut off before he could reach the wall. The other guard's sheets rose over his head and hit him in the face.

The two of them searched all over the room. Then they tried the light switch on the wall again. Those yellow lights, every time they switched on in the middle of the dark forest, were blinding in the valley. Alec could hear their shouting even from inside the house.

"She's doing her stuff," Daisie quipped. "Whatever she did, she spooked the hell out of... They're—" Daisie pointed at the inner balcony. "Look! Look over there, Alec! Look at them go!"

But Alec was watching someone run down the stairs. From the cliffside, he could only make out a short section of the second floor and it was hard to discern, but it had to be Reggie.

"No, no, the driveway, Alec," Daisie said, pointing. "Look over at the driveway in the front!"

Alec heard the car ignition before he saw anything. And with it came more shouting. They were far enough away that the shouting was muffled. An old Dodge Challenger appeared, skidding along the driveway. It nearly ran off the road into a ravine then sped down the windy road to the main highway.

"She did it, Alec!" Daisie exclaimed, putting her arm around him. "She did it! They're running!"

Daisie hit his shoulder again and pointed at Reggie, tripping along the driveway in the front yard, yanking up his pants, shouting like crazy. When his pants were up, he raised his fists. He was shouting for them to come back, but his friends were long gone.

But then…everything stilled. The sound of crickets seemed loud. And soon the lights in the living room shut off.

He heard the crunching of leaves. Then Joy's immaculate bare feet materialized on the trail up to the summit of their hill. That was followed by the rest of her materializing in her usual blouse and jeans. She approached and, standing over them, she frowned. She seemed so down.

She dropped two pistols on the ground.

"Here," she said solemnly. "At least there's that. I tried, I really did. But I told you Reggie isn't going anywhere."

"What are you talking about?" asked Daisie. "We saw them running."

"You saw his guards running," Joy said. "We need Reggie to run, not just hired help. I told you I couldn't frighten him. He's not going to run from an investment just because its haunted."

"Did you show Reggie Fifi's face?" asked Alec.

"No."

"Why not?"

"Reggie was smoking on the balcony when I messed with his friends."

"Why didn't you scare him when he was out on the balcony?"

"*Cause I died on the balcony, dummy!* Can you explain this to your dense friend, Daisie! Jeesh. You can be so fucking out of it sometimes, Alec. Maybe…shit, maybe…we'll try again tomorrow."

But then Joy turned back to the trail and headed down the hillside, looking depressed as hell. She just shook her head and disappeared.

"I'm sorry, Joy," Alec said. "Sorry."

"Whatever," Joy hollered back in the wind. "You can be so insensitive sometimes."

"We need to go home too, Alec," Daisie said. "It's getting cold."

"Wait, Joy. Don't go."

She didn't answer.

"We could still get rid of him if she'd just try again now," Alec said to Daisie. "All she has to do is just show him Fifi's face."

"Alec, forget it. She can't now. We'll try again tomorrow."

THE BROKEN RECORD

THE NEXT EVENING THE PLAN WAS SIMPLE AND straightforward enough: Joy would haunt Reggie again. Alec and Daisie went outside with her, under the cover of darkness, amidst thick undergrowth. Standing close to the kitchen glass door, they were cold. Alec had thought it would be a little warmer close to the house than on the peak of Plymouth Crest. At least they had come better prepared, wearing heavier coats. But it was still frigid.

The cold was the only thing reminding Alec that Joy was a ghost. It had never seemed to bother her until now. She started trembling. Or maybe that was fear. She also looked scared.

"Do your thing, Joy," Alec whispered. "We'll be standing down here waiting for you."

Joy nodded hesitantly.

"What's the matter?" asked Daisie. "You seem worried."

"It's like the time I opened for Madison Square Park, right guys? I used to be so nervous performing in big venues. I loved it when I was finally up on stage, but that sea of seats made me totally freak out. Maybe it's like that?

Right? But…what if he's on the balcony again, Alec? I don't know if I can go up there."

"You have to scare him tonight," Alec said. "Otherwise, he'll bring reinforcements. Besides, we already looked. He's not up on the terrace."

"All you can do is try," Daisie said, rubbing Joy's back.

"I know. I know. Thanks."

"If anything happens, I'll run inside," Alec said. "Come on. Face him. This is the house *you* built, not his." And he put an arm around her again and squeezed her.

"Why don't you turn into your monster *this* time?" whispered Daisie with a smirk. "It sure worked on me."

"Reggie would laugh," Joy said with a chuckle. "But I think I've got a better idea. I just have to get the nerve to do it." She nodded and met Alec's gaze again. "Okay, Alec. I'm ready. I'll get my house back for you."

"Not for me. For you, Joy."

"For you, Alec," she said with a smile, shaking her head. "For you."

And then Joy dematerialized.

Then it fell quiet. And Alec and Daisie were left shivering beside thick tree trunks, keeping vigil beside the kitchen door.

"It's really just as cold here as at the top of the cliff," Daisie whispered with teeth chattering. "Brrr. We should head home. There's nothing we're going to be able to do to help her."

"I thought it'd be warmer closer to the house."

"Not tonight. It's freezing tonight. I know you want to be here for her, but there's nothing we can do. She's a ghost. But, still… I like her a lot. And she said that asshole abused and killed her. I hope whatever she does, she gets even with that jerk."

Alec nodded.

Then they jumped. A scream was coming from right

above them, on the balcony. They ran out in the open, risking being seen, and gazed up at the terrace. The light turned on in the bedroom, seeming to illuminate the whole forest, but Alec couldn't find anyone up there.

"That didn't sound like Reggie," said Alec.

"It sounded like Joy!" Daisie said.

Alec ran to the kitchen door, rustling for the keys in his pocket.

"Stop, Alec! Stop. She's a ghost. What are you going to do for her?"

"*Joy!*" thundered Reggie.

It sounded like it was right above them. He realized it must be coming from upstairs. And that jerk sounded far more pissed than scared.

"*Fuck you, Reggie!*" shouted Joy, sounding as if she was crying. "*Fuck you! Leave me alone! I came here to get away from you! You ruined me!*"

"*I ruined you? Me?*"

"*She sounds like she's in trouble!*" Alec said.

"Alec, think!" Daisie insisted, pulling at his arm. "How can a ghost be in trouble?"

"I don't know," he said. "I don't know. But I'm not going to stay outside and listen. I have to try to help her."

He finally managed the lock on the kitchen door and then, forgetting all stealth, he threw it open. Then he ran across his dark living room and rushed to the stairway.

"*I ruined you?*" Reggie shouted. "*No, no, no, you ruined me! You ruined all of us hiding in this shithole. Why? Why here, Joy? Hey, you, come back now. You come back! No! Come back to me! You—*"

"*I'm happy for once! Okay, Reggie? I like it here. Now, stay the fuck away from me!*"

Alec climbed two or three steps at a time and ran around the balcony toward the bedroom.

"You want to stay?" asked Reggie. "Fine. Not sure how it'll help your career. I can move in with you."

"You'll never move here, Reggie." Joy laughed derisively. "Why do you think I chose this place? There's no way in hell you, Travis, Jenny, or any of the others will come here. That's why it's so wonderful."

"You bitch! I made you what you are."

There were slapping sounds. It sounded like he was hitting her!

"*Go away!*"

"*Joy!*" Alec cried, finally rushing into the bedroom.

But then he stumbled back to the threshold. The light was bright, unnaturally bright, turning the whole room yellow. Then Alec nearly fell, witnessing the impossible. There were two Reggies in the room. Reggie "one" was far younger than the Reggie Alec remembered, wearing a black T-shirt, sports jacket, and slacks and without a mustache. He was attacking Joy in the center of the room. The other Reggie, the Reggie who threw Alec out of his house the other day, was wearing only pajama bottoms. He crouched by the bed, with eyes wide open, staring at the spectacle. He was in so much shock that he hadn't even seemed to notice Alec barging into the room.

"*Get the hell away from me!*" Joy shouted again. "*Don't touch me!*"

But Joy wasn't Joy either. She had Fifi's face, wearing a white beret and sweater, shouting, as the other Reggie— Reggie number one—rushed her toward the glass door that opened onto the outside terrace.

"*Go away!*" Joy screamed.

"*Are you drunk again? Is that it!*"

"I don't need alcohol," she said, wiping her eyes, laughing derisively again. "Not where I'm happy. Just stay —" She batted his hands away. "No! No! Don't you touch me! Just stay away from me. I told you not to touch—"

"Joy, I came here to marry you!"

They were on the terrace now. He reached for Joy's hand again, but she slapped it off her.

"I'd rather die than marry you!"

"Bitch, calm down!"

"Calm yourself! And…and…just go away!"

Joy, or Fifi, lost her balance, falling backward, and her whole torso tipped over the concrete ledge. For a moment, only her legs were keeping her from falling. Reggie tried to grab her arm, but she slipped through his fingers and tumbled backward over the ledge.

Reggie stared over the concrete ledge.

"Oh my God," Reggie said in a broken voice. But it wasn't the Reggie gazing over the wall. The Reggie on the balcony was simply staring down. The comment came from the one in pajamas by the bed.

"You bitch! I made you what you are."

Joy materialized in the center of the bedroom with tears streaming from her eyes. But her face, again, was not Joy's, it was Fifi's. Reggie had chased her in from the hallway—the younger clean-shaven Reggie, again, in his black T-shirt and sports jacket. He struck her a few times viciously across the face, making her stumble to the floor. Then he slugged and kicked her a few times and pulled her hair. She forced herself up, backing away from him.

"Go away!" she cried. *"Get the hell away from me!"* Joy, or Fifi in her white beret and sweater, shouted again. *"Don't touch me! Go away!"*

"Are you drunk again? Is that it!"

"I don't need alcohol," she said, wiping her eyes, laughing. "Not where I'm happy. Just stay—" She batted his hands away on the balcony. "No! No! Don't you touch me! Just stay away from me. I told you not to touch—"

"Joy, I came here to marry you."

He reached for her hand again and she batted it away.

"I'd rather die than marry you!"

"Bitch, you calm down!"

"Calm yourself! And…and…just *go away!*"

Joy, or Fifi, lost her balance, falling backward, and her whole torso tipped over the concrete ledge. For a moment, only her legs were keeping her from falling. Reggie tried to grab her arm, but she slipped through his fingers and tumbled backward over the ledge. All over again.

Reggie stared over the concrete wall.

"My God," Reggie said quietly, shaking his head. "My God, please stop this. Please. Stop this. Please."

~

"You bitch! I made you what you are."

And Joy was back in the center of the bedroom with Fifi's face. Once again, Reggie stormed in from the hall— Reggie, the younger clean-shaven Reggie, again, in his black T-shirt and sports jacket. He struck Joy over and over, until she stumbled to the floor.

"*Go away!*" Joy, or Fifi, shouted again leaping back up. "*Get the hell away from me! Go away!*"

"It keeps happening over and over," Reggie said by the bed, shaking his head. "Why?" He stumbled on the bed. "Why?" He put his head in his hands. "Why doesn't it stop?" And tears fell from Reggie's eyes too. "Please make it stop."

"Alec?" cried Daisie, rushing into the bedroom.

"I'm happy here," she said, wiping her eyes, laughing derisively again. "Just stay—" She batted his hands away.

"No! No! Don't you touch me! Just stay away from me. I told you not to touch—"

And now Daisie, standing in the doorway, was watching the fight too. Over and over it kept playing like a broken record. Joy would appear in the middle of the room. But it wasn't Joy, it was Fifi. Then Reggie would attack her. Joy would get up, and then he'd chase her to the open door onto the terrace. Rushing her, he'd try to stop her, but she'd trip and fall over the ledge to her death. And once she fell, it would start up all over again. Over and over and over again.

"I don't understand what's going on," said Alec.

"She's haunting him," said Daisie. "She's showing him what he did to her. Good for her. If that asshole ever lets it sink in."

Reggie leaned over the mattress. It seemed he wanted to look away, but he couldn't. *"Go away,"* he said, shaking his head with a nervous laugh. He looked at Alec but seemed to look through him. *"Go away."*

"Cabin fever, Alec," Daisie said with a big smile. "I told you this house does that to people sometimes. Or shock. Whatever the case, we can get him the hell out of your house now."

"Throw him out of my house now, guys!" shouted Joy in a disembodied voice.

Meanwhile, Fifi was being pushed to her death. Again. Over and over and over again…haunting Reginald again and again.

PASS THE MASHED POTATOES

ALEC AND DAISIE SAT ACROSS FROM ONE ANOTHER ON white leather seats at a tiny wooden kitchen table near Daisie's kitchen. Alec wore a pressed brown suit. Daisie was formal in a very pretty draping dark green floral dress. But they weren't on a date this time. They were meeting as "family."

After Alec uncovered the meat, stuffing, potatoes, and vegetable trays, he poured gravy over his and Daisie's sliced turkey. Then he sat down.

"This is so wonderful, Alec," Daisie said. She reached over the table to touch his hands. "Thanks so much for picking it up, especially with the weather turning so icy. I'd kind of rather you didn't, honestly, but you know I can't cook. Going to Badger in the snow must have been so difficult."

"I saw two cars off the side of the road just on the way over," he said, nodding and chewing on a roll. "Another had turned three-sixty on the road on the way back. Thank God it didn't look like anyone was hurt. A police officer had his patrol car with its red and blue lights flashing in the middle of the highway, slowing down traffic. Traffic is one thing I never thought I'd see here around Plymouth Hill. But"—He forked some turkey into his mouth—"the cop was familiar enough. Sheriff Denson. When he saw me directing traffic, he hollered *'Happy Thanksgiving.'*" You know, as much as we poke fun at him, he told me he works every holiday season."

"Who else is gonna take his shifts?"

"That's my point." Alec shrugged, chewing on stuffing. "He's not so bad, is he? Last week, I passed by the police station, and he told me that if Reggie ever returns, he'll chase him away for me. Of course, all it would take is documents showing Reggie's ownership and suddenly Denson would be saying he can't do anything again."

He sipped some white wine.

"You still haven't seen her?" asked Daisie.

"Hmm? Who?"

He cut some turkey with his fork and knife.

"You know who," she said. "You still haven't seen her since she haunted Reggie?"

"No."

And that made that familiar sense of unease return. He felt deflated. Daisie frowned.

"Oh, I'm so sorry, Alec," Daisie muttered.

"Yeah." He shrugged. "Well, I don't get why. I've called her name aloud a million times, but she won't show up. I've even walked around the lake and the hills in the snow shouting out her name. There's no sign of her. But she's disappeared before. She always comes back..." He shrugged. "God, I miss her, Daisie. God...if she's really gone, it's terrible. But if she is, I just wish...I could have said goodbye."

Daisie reached over and touched his hand again.

"If she can see me, I know she'll show up again," Alec said. He forced himself to spoon some mashed potatoes into his mouth. "I know she will. She'd at least say goodbye."

"How about the legal stuff?" she asked. "Do you at least finally have possession of the house?"

Alec looked up at her and was amused by the moon sketched on her forehead. She always changed the drawing to match the current phase of the moon. Tonight the moon was apparently full, but with all the clouds outside, he could only tell by looking at her head.

"I'm firing Chip," he said with a chuckle, cutting more meat. "He's a good friend, but makes a lousy realtor."

"That's not what I asked," she said with a chuckle. "You should have done that a long time ago. Who owns the house now, Alec?"

"Joy. She's always owned her house."

And that's when she appeared. She materialized in her usual dark blouse and jeans, standing over them by the small table.

"Joy!"

Alec leapt up and took her in his arms—but she stepped back. From the corner of his eye, Alec saw a wooden cabinet open and a crystal wine glass and plate float to the table and land beside Alec's plate. Then their bottle of white wine lifted itself and filled Joy's empty glass, while a matching white leather chair from a corner of the house by the bathroom slid over.

Joy sat down beside Alec.

"Can you pass the mashed potatoes?" Joy asked, heaving a sigh.

"It's so good to see you, Joy," Daisie said.

"It's great seeing you!" Alec echoed, sitting back down.

"Hi, Alec," Joy said with a chuckle. "Daisie. It's so great seeing you guys again." But she seemed depressed. She raised her wine glass, forced a smile, and toasted them. Then Joy sipped it (but she didn't drink any, she just pretended). "To friends. Happy Thanksgiving. It's nice to spend this special time together."

"Where have you been?" Alec asked.

"Wait," Joy said, raising her palm. "So, um—" She sipped more wine. "How will you keep the house, Alec? If you know Reggie like I do, he'll be back."

"After what you did to him?" asked Daisie.

"You don't know Reggie. He doesn't like heights, but he'd climb Mount Everest if it meant making money. Even if he has to come back in a straightjacket, he'll be back." She laughed. "Yeah, I scared him good though, didn't I? But for only so long. Trust me. The mighty dollar always brings that jerk back. Still—" She tapped her red fingernails on her wine glass. She wagged a finger. "I think I've got a plan."

"You always had the plans," Daisie said, sipping some wine. "You were the one who threw him out."

"Yeah," Joy said with a thin smile. "Sure did. But I couldn't have done that without you and Alec. You guys gave me the courage to do it."

She turned to Alec with a rueful grin. There was something about that smile that really hurt—a smile he had longed for so much these past few days, but now it seemed so sad.

"You two gave me the strength," Joy said. "That's what this day is all about, you know. Giving thanks to the people you love."

"Where've you been, Joy?" Alec asked again. "I've been calling out your name everywhere. I wandered around the house, went up to the top of the hill, even hiked all around the lake calling out your name a thousand times. I've missed you so much and—"

"Wait," Joy said again, raising a hand. She shook her head and stared up at the ceiling for a moment. "Wait… just wait one second… I know you did." She looked back at him and flashed a grin. "I have an idea to finally straighten things out. See, I've been signing checks with the bank for years. I've sent checks for taxes and the mortgage on the place, just like I did when I was alive. To the world, maybe not my fans, but to the banks, Josephine Graynger is alive. I was never pronounced dead. So, I figure, why not use my signature one final time and transfer the deed of the house to you? That way Reggie won't vie for control of our place anymore. He won't be able to, legally. And then if the brute comes back, our sheriff can actually be of help for once."

"But you'd need a notary to make it legal," Daisie said.

"Doesn't Plymouth Hill's Corner Store have a notary?" Joy asked.

"Hey, how did you know I was a notary, Joy?" Daisie said, slapping the table.

"Been snooping around for a while," Joy said with a shrug and smirk.

"But why didn't you give it to Alec in the first place?" Daisie asked.

"Well—" She turned back to Alec and frowned. "I really don't think I wanted to give my place up. Even to you, Alec. You don't know how mad I was when Reggie's ditzy son had movers take my stuff away. Nobody really knows how hard it is to give things you love away until you pass away."

"Sure, you can hand it all over to me," Alec said with a big smile. "Sure, Joy. That'd work for both of us now."

"No, Alec, it won't work for *us*," she snapped, shaking her head. "That's what I'm trying to tell you."

"What do you mean?" asked Alec, furrowing his brow. He reached over to squeeze her hand, but her hand singed him like an open flame.

"*Fuck! Damn it, Alec!*" She slammed her fist on the table. "*Stop touching my hand! Why do you keep doing that! How many times do I have to—*"

"Sorry."

"*He's so dense, Daisie!*" Joy exclaimed. "So dense! What the hell's wrong with him?" But then she looked down, shaking her head, and chuckled. "Like, he doesn't get I'm a ghost. I guess it's kinda cute." She heaved a sigh. "Alec, you'll take my home. It's yours. That will take care of all your problems in Plymouth Hill."

"But you can still stay in the house with me."

"Not after I give the house away."

"Why?"

She gazed into his eyes for a moment. Then a tear fell from her eye. That tear stung his heart more than the burning her hand ever did.

She quickly turned back to the table and served herself some turkey with a fork from the open silver box. She cut and sliced a piece. Then she pretended to sip more white wine.

"Who chose the wine?" Joy asked, swallowing.

"Me," Daisie said.

"I bet you have really good taste, Daisie. I wish I could taste it."

"Why do you look like someone—"

"Like someone died, Alec?" Joy snapped, pretending to sip more wine. "Like someone died? Hmm? Why do I look like someone who died? Cause I did. And I think it's about time you realize that." She looked angry, but her comment brought even more tears streaming from her eyes. Then, with a measured voice, she said, "Shit. All right…well, you see, Alec, I now know the reason I was haunting my house. It had always been about Reggie. All ghosts haunt things when trying to fix past traumas. I read it"—She cupped her hand, winking at him and gesturing to Daisie—"I snuck into the witch aisle of her store and read some witchcraft books on the end of life."

"Joy!" Daisie snapped.

"Sorry," Joy said with a shrug.

"Anyway, a haunting, I learned," Joy continued, "means repeating over and over again, and it's done by spirits that feel like their lives need something that's been left unfulfilled. My situation was obvious. I had lost my dream, ripped from me by my manager and agent. Worse, I thought I had escaped him and finally found happiness on Plymouth Crest. He stole that happiness from me when I died, just like he had when I was living in L.A. Well, with your help, I fixed it. You guys gave me the nerve to finally do what I had to do to Reggie."

She looked pensively toward the small window for a moment. Then she looked pained.

"Can you explain the rest, Daisie?" Joy said finally, with her voice breaking. "Alec is sweet, but he can be so dense… you know, and I don't think I can keep going on. Fuck… fuck… I hate byes so much, just like I hate cries." She glanced at Alec and wiped tears with the back of her hand. "Just, you go tell him the rest, Daisie."

"You're leaving me," Alec said somberly.

"Yes, Alec," Joy said. "Yes. I have to. You love my house? Well, now you can have it. You can live happily ever after here." Then she looked down at her plate and sort of swirled her mashed potatoes. "I fucking love mashed potatoes, guys. Just as I loved drinking orange juice with you that morning, Alec. God, I'm going to miss you so much. Just like I'm going to miss this special night with my friends in Plymouth Hill. Thanksgiving with family is something I didn't have when I was alive. It's so special."

Joy raised her wine glass to toast, but her hand shook. Daisie raised her glass too.

Alec didn't. He felt horrible.

"Did you finish your book?" Joy asked Alec, throwing her long hair back and bringing more wine to her lips.

Then she brought the plate closer and cut some turkey with a fork and knife.

"I don't care about my book."

"She has to go, Alec," Daisie said.

"How the hell would you know, Daisie," Alec snapped. "Some witch you are, you probably didn't even read the book she's talking about."

"Now you're being mean," warned Joy.

"More like woman's intuition," Daisie muttered. Daisie's voice cracked. She was on the verge of crying too.

"It's taking all my effort to spend this little time left with you," Joy said quietly, trying hard to force a smile. "I only came back to make the transfer of my deed official. You notarize my signature, Daisie. Then I can go. God, sorry… it all sounds awful. I'm sorry, I really am. Oh, Alec, if this was only about you, it'd be different."

"What is it about?"

"It's hard to explain."

"Try me."

"I want to go," Joy said. "If you saw what I saw, you'd want to leave too. So…" Joy cut some meat. She chewed. (But she was pretending. The meat remained on the fork.) "I came by to say goodbye to my friends. I love you guys so much. I'll sign the deed to Alec, Daisie will notarize it, and we'll be done with this whole debacle. Reggie will have to stay far away, where he belongs. And we all will live, or die, happily ever after."

Then they returned to quietly eating. Only the sounds of dishes clinking and forks and knives moving were heard. And Joy seemed content just pretending to eat and drink with them.

"I don't get it," Alec finally said, running his hand through his hair. "You can give me the house legally and still stay there. No one will know. Why don't you stay in the house with me? You like me. You told me you *loved* me. Why would you want to leave me?"

"She said she wants to go, Alec," Daisie said, wiping tears. "She said her haunting's over."

"*She's not done haunting me!*" Alec snapped, slapping the table hard.

That quieted everyone all over again. Daisie and Joy just froze, staring down at the table.

"I never liked your temper," Joy muttered quietly. "You're not making things any better, Alec."

"I'm...sorry," Alec said solemnly. "Sorry, Joy. Sorry, Daisie."

"It's okay, Alec," Daisie said.

"Let's try to enjoy these last moments together," Joy said.

But that was an awful thing to say. Joy raised the wine glass once more, and they all toasted each other and forced a smile.

SNOW, SNOW, AND MORE SNOW

Chip stood at the living room window, staring outside as icy flurries fell on trees and shrubs, covering everything in Alec's backyard with a white blanket. Sipping from a small cocktail glass, he peered upstairs through the second-floor window. He kept shaking his head. Alec wasn't sure if it was out of rage or if he was in awe of his view. Maybe both? All the while, Alec sat on his black leather sofa, typing the last chapter of his novel on his laptop. Normally, he wouldn't type with company, but this was Chip's fourth day staying at his house.

"Well, Merry Christmas," Chip said, heaving a sigh. "Suppose vengeance is yours. Inviting me to your house only to get me trapped here."

"I didn't know," Alec said, shaking his head. "Really, I didn't. Sorry. But thanks for coming."

"Fuck you," Chip said, shaking his head. "Really. Fuck off, man. Cheryl is expecting me back home for the holidays, you jerk. If this snow keeps up, I won't make it back in time."

"Your family will understand."

"They won't." Chip turned around.

He walked away and angrily plopped back down in a chair. But then he grinned and pointed at Alec with the hand holding his cocktail glass. "I don't really get you, Alec. How and why did you decide that you want to live here? It's so boring. Oh, it's that writing thing, right?"

"It's amazing here," Alec said, shrugging and typing more.

"Let's talk about our deal," Chip said, leaning forward in the chair. "You're really going to pay me 10 percent off the original asking price? Why? Is this my Christmas present?"

"Merry Christmas," Alec said, looking up with a smirk.

"Mind telling me the secret of how you got this incredible deal? Did you send some commandos in to get rid of Reginald and commandeer the mansion? More importantly, how did you have Fifi Graynger sign the house over to you? A *dead* Fifi Graynger."

"If I told you, you wouldn't believe me."

"She's not dead? That's it, isn't it?"

A shadow crossed the kitchen door. Alec stopped typing and stared. He thought, or hoped, that it wasn't just outside the window. He so hoped it was Joy. He had hoped his ghost would appear every day since she left two weeks ago. But the shadow came and went as fast as it had appeared. It was probably just a bird in the branches.

Chip was still staring at him.

"You found Fifi?" Chip said. "That's it, right? Fifi Graynger is alive, like some of her fans guessed, and she sold her house to you, but you swore to never tell anybody. That's why you won't tell me—even though I'm your best friend."

"Not exactly," Alec said with a chuckle. "Or, I suppose...well—"

Chip gesticulated for more information.

"Does it matter?" Alec asked.

"No." Chip sipped more whiskey and shook his head. "Not if you're giving me 10 percent." He sank deeper in the lounge chair. "Hey, are there any restaurants around here? Or do I have to keep eating your frozen food?"

"Frozen. Nearest restaurant is—"

"Three hundred miles by the nearest airport."

"I'm really sorry, Chip," Alec said with a laugh. "Really I am. I didn't know the roads would close. Daisie told me this snowstorm hit a bit early this year. She said the road will probably still reopen by Christmas."

"Probably?" Chip said, jumping up. "*Fuck, you did this on purpose!*"

"I didn't," Alec said with a laugh.

"Alec, I'm telling you, I mean, I guarantee, I promise you, I will slush my rental Toyota through ice, sleet, and then down the frickin' hill itself, if I have to, to get back to the airport and fly home."

Chip frowned. But after he sipped more whiskey, he smirked at him.

The doorbell rang. Chip jumped up, probably excited to see *anyone*. Alec followed, knowing who it was before Chip opened the door.

"Hey, Alec," Daisie said, in her red coat and hat, reaching for a hug. She handed him a large bag of groceries. "I waited till the snow quieted to get you all this stuff. These flurries are so early this year."

"Are the roads open?" Chip asked.

"Not yet." Daisie laughed. "It took me an hour just to get up Alec's hill." Then she handed Alec her coat and hat and walked inside. She shook Chip's hand. "I'm Daisie. You're one of his foreigner friends from the other side of the country?"

"Chip," he said with a nod.

"Oh, you're *Chip*," Daisie said disdainfully. "You're the realtor."

"Hey!" Chip snapped, turning to Alec. "What the hell did you tell her about me? What does she mean by looking all disgusted when saying *the realtor*?"

"I told her you're my realtor. Did I need to say anything else?"

They all laughed.

"You can't get on the roads yet, Chip," Daisie said. "You'll have to wait just a couple more days. I drove slow, real slow, with chains up the hill, but I've been stranded a couple times. At least Alec's hillside is not too curvy or steep, so if I slip down the hill, I don't crash to my death, I just land in a ditch. But I wouldn't be driving anywhere farther than Plymouth Hill."

"Great," Chip said.

"You came just in time, Daisie," Alec said. "You can talk to him. I've just been writing, and he's bored as hell by me."

"He gets really boring when he writes," Daisie said with a chuckle. "Well…" She hooked Chip by the arm and walked with him into the living room. "I work the Corner Store at the bottom of the hill, so, if you're looking for supplies this week, Chip, look no further. I don't have much business this time of the year, so you can have my personal "Daisie" delivery service. I've got plenty of windshield ice scrapers and spare shovels." She laughed again. "So, tell me, how long have you and Alec been friends? I feel bad Alec drew you all the way here for the winter."

"This house was quite a good deal for me," Chip said, shaking his head.

"I thought you fired him?" Daisie asked with a smirk, looking back at Alec.

Alec shrugged.

Alec walked to the entryway to close the door, but before he shut it, he thought he saw something heading up the snow-covered hiking trail. At first, he thought it was a deer. But then he noted only two legs. And the lady wore a blue coat with a fur collar. That was the jacket Joy wore when she first met him in the kitchen.

"Joy!" Alec said, running outside. "Joy? Joy!"

Alec rushed onto his snowy driveway. It was so frigid and he was just in a T-shirt and sweats with slippers. He didn't care, as long as Joy was back. He'd fight a blizzard all the way up to the top of the hill for a chance to see her again. But as he gazed at the trail, going farther up the hill, now covered in a foot of snow, she faded away.

"Alec," Daisie said behind him. "Alec, come back inside! Are you crazy? It's so cold outside."

"I saw her! I saw Joy, Daisie! I'm sure of it. She came back!"

"She told you," Daisie said, shaking her head. "She left for good. Now come back inside before you freeze to death."

THE NEW YEAR

Alec sat on his white plastic chair in a coat. Although snow still covered the leaves and branches below, it was warm enough to sit on the terrace that he loved so much. The sky was hazy and there was a pleasant smell of snow, but the clouds weren't as dark and foreboding as yesterday. At the bottom of the hill, about a foot of snow had accumulated over his patio. The roof provided some cover over his terrace, but he'd still had to clear ice from all the windows before he'd started writing this morning. There was a constant dripping sound of water running down the slope of his roof. In the distance was the iced-over lake. It was a bit dark without the sun's glow, but the vista over the woods was breathtaking, as always.

This week marked the new year, and it meant good tidings. Alec had managed to stay in Plymouth Crest until winter. Daisie had wagered he'd be gone by now. And Chip had left Plymouth Crest and made it back home for Christmas.

But there was a negative side to the new year. January first had heralded his deadline to finish his novel. He was supposed to have had the manuscript in his editor's hands last month. So he finally did what he really didn't want to do. He called his agent.

"Happy new year, Phoebe."

"Hey, Alec. Happy new year! Your house buried in snow yet?"

"Snow's thick and it's very cold, but the view is still stunning. The house is gorgeous. How's the rest of your gang back home?"

"Great. Great. Family's great. Look, I'm going to send you the cover for your new book. The artist we got is amazing. The image is bright, like you requested, with a yellow tint to mark the sun's rays. For the back, the publisher was thinking it'd be good to get some pictures of our bestselling author. You keep telling me how amazing your town is, so why not let your readers see who their writer is with that lake and forest of yours as a backdrop? Can you send me some photos of you beside your amazing home?"

"Sure I can."

"Did you make a decision about coming back to L.A. to do a book tour?"

"I'm going to try to make it back there to see my grandson born. But I told my daughter that I won't be able to go if I'm snowed in. She's not due for another month. But with the weather, I really don't think we should plan a tour, Phoebe."

"If you change your mind, I need to schedule the dates with stores as soon as possible. You know, people prefer seeing you in person."

"I wouldn't schedule anything now."

"Hmm, you never liked public appearances."

"Yeah. Listen, I've got some bad news."

That led to silence. After a month's delay, Alec didn't think he needed to say much else.

"What is it with you lately, Alec? You never had writer's

block before? Maybe this middle of nowhere stuff isn't helping your writing career like you thought it would?"

"I just need another month for the final chapter. Promise."

"The editors have a schedule too."

"Just one more month. I promise. I just need to finish this last chapter."

"Alec, you can write a chapter in an hour."

"Just one more month."

Phoebe went silent again.

Alec jumped up and stood closer to the concrete ledge, just staring out at the lake below. He wandered a bit too close to the ledge with a sudden terror of falling. That was the first time he realized why the ledge was so shallow. Joy had built it low so as not to obstruct the view. She had loved this view so much that she had died for it.

Phoebe heaved a sigh.

"Please, just one month," he repeated.

"We might have to delay the launch. But you only need one chapter? I don't get it. Just write the goddamn chapter, Alec."

"I think I can make the story so much better. At least two more weeks. Please."

"Fine," she said with a sigh. "Happy new year, Alec. We'll make do, as we always do. I can't wait to read your novel."

And she hung up her phone.

Then Alec sat back down in his chair and stared out at the view again. Yes, maybe it was too beautiful for writing. But now he had bought himself a little more time to enjoy it.

He forced himself to do some typing—just when the cellphone buzzed again in his pocket. He expected Chip, or his agent again, but it was his daughter.

"Daddy?"

"Hey, Rachel. Happy new year!"

"Thanks, Dad. Happy new year. I tried to reach you yesterday but your phone was down."

"It was probably snowing too hard. You know how the reception is when it gets stormy here."

"Well, Dad, my water broke so I'm in the hospital now. The baby might come at any moment, and you insisted I call you and let you know when that happened."

"I'll be right over!"

"What?" she asked. "Wait…what? Wait, you're really gonna fly all the way over now? But I know how far away you live. And you said it's been storming. Isn't it snowing there? I'm just calling because I promised to let you know."

"Never mind, I'll be right there, Rachel. You're at the hospital already? Wow. This is so early. So sorry about yesterday, babe, it's just that when the clouds are thick, the phones—"

"Just be careful, Dad. I'd love it if you came, sure, but don't do it if the roads are too dangerous. Please, just be careful."

"I'm so happy for you, babe."

"Me too. I'm really excited. It's going to be wonderful. I'm getting contractions a lot. The doctor says the baby could come anywhere from a few hours till tomorrow morning. They already checked with an ultrasound, and everything seems to be going fine. I'm just a little nervous. It's really exciting."

"You'll be fine. I'll—"

It was then, further down the hillside, surrounded by snow-covered trees, that a woman appeared. The lady was staring out at the lake, wearing a dark shawl and pants. The same clothes she had worn on that first day he had visited the house.

It was Joy!

"Babies come when babies come, I suppose," Rachel said.

"I'll… I'll be right there, Rachel," Alec stammered, jumping up. "But I have to go now, babe. I'm so happy for you. I'll see you soon."

"I love you, Daddy." She hung up the phone.

"Joy!" Alec hollered and waved. "Joy! Are you back?"

She shook her head slowly, wrapping her arms around herself, as if feeling cold. But he caught a smile from her profile—Joy's smile, the smile he had fallen in love with and missed so much.

But she wouldn't turn.

"Joy!"

She just stood there with her arms wrapped around herself in her dark shawl and jeans, barefoot, staring out at the icy lake. The sun peeked through a cloud, and rays of sunlight reflected off the lake. That gold light shimmered over Joy's face.

"Joy, answer me. Come on. Joy!"

Alec rushed back inside, ran around the inner balcony, and dashed down the stairs. But when he threw the front door open, she was gone.

RACHEL

Alec walked through the double glass doors of the hospital, past a reception desk, and then into an elevator. He checked his cellphone. Somehow, he had made it back to California in less than a day. Somehow. He'd had to. But he was exhausted. He had driven through treacherous, slippery, and icy roads with his Lexus, sliding some of the way, for the three-hundred miles to the airport, and all the way, other cars had been stranded off the road in the thick snowfall. Then came the lines in the airport and the flight itself. There were threats of delays. But he would get there to see his daughter, somehow. Somehow, he'd make it for the delivery of his grandson. With his heart beating hard in his chest, excited, now walking fast down a hallway, he was finally on his way to the hospital room number she had texted him.

He didn't make it. That is, he didn't make it in time for her delivery.

Rachel lay in bed, in a blue hospital gown, exhausted, with a baby lying on her chest. His daughter looked weak and pale, but she smiled when he entered the room.

"Where's Matt?" Alec asked, looking around.

"He stepped out for breakfast, Dad." Then she smiled and nodded at the baby on her chest. "Daniel. Your grandson. Isn't he wonderful, Daddy?"

"He sure is."

"Do you want to hold him?"

Alec carefully lifted up his grandson, wrapped in a baby blue blanket. His eyes were closed. He was quietly sleeping. Alec gently kissed those chubby cheeks and rocked him a little. Then he gently laid him back down carefully in his mother's arms.

"I'm so proud of you, Rachel." He kissed his daughter's cheek. "Wow. He's so cute."

"I…" She tried to sit up on the hospital bed, but Alec gestured for her to stay put. Instead, he sat beside her on the bed, holding her hand. "I felt bad calling you. Matt said asking you to be here was a dumb idea. But I told him you insisted I call when the baby was coming. But he's right. You just live too far away. And it's snowing, right? I wasn't thinking straight, but I just—"

"I don't care. I'm so glad I came."

"Well, we still need to come and see your place. We so want to visit."

"When you're well. I'd love you to see the house. I'd love for Danny to see it too."

"Hey, Rache, brought you a bagel," a man said, barging into the room. "If you're hungry. The cafeteria was busy. I heard—"

"Oh," Matt said. He walked over and gave Alec a hug. "This is a surprise. Wow. Hi, Dad."

"Hi Matt. Congratulations."

"Thanks," Matt said putting an arm around Alec. "Congratulations to you, grandpa." He laughed. "It was so sudden, right? She kept talking about how she kinda wanted to run postterm just so you'd be able to come for sure after winter. Came preterm instead. Man, you came all the way here from your place? You live so far. You staying in a hotel?"

"He's staying with us, dummy," Rachel replied.

"Oh, of course," Matt said with a chuckle.

"I hope I can return the favor soon," Alec said, "and you two can come visit when the winter's over. We were just talking about that. You two bring the baby. You'd all love it there."

"I saw how beautiful your house is," Rachel said with a nod.

"We kept checking out the pictures together," Matt said with a nod. "It's incredible, Dad. What a gem. I can't wait to visit."

Then Matt sat by Rachel's side in the same place Alec had a moment earlier. He took her hand. But the baby opened his eyes and started fussing, so Rachel started opening her gown to breastfeed.

That's when a nurse walked into the room. She looked at the plastic wires and machines by the bedside. Then she looked down on Rachel and the baby smiling. She reached for Daniel and transferred him to a wheeled bassinet.

"Kiddo will be right back," the nurse said.

"You made it just in time to see him, Dad," Rachel said. "They're gonna take Daniel away just for a little bit."

"He'll be right back," the nurse repeated.

"He looks so cute, Rachel," Alec said. "I'm so proud of you. So happy for both of you."

"I think Mom would have really loved him," she said with a nod.

JOY

Traveling back home was not nearly as easy as flying to California. When he landed, the snowstorms had only gotten worse. There was zero visibility, and Daisie had suggested on the phone that Alec stay away for a month. Daisie offered to watch over his place, but Alec wanted to be home nearly as much as he had wanted to be there for his daughter (and, secretly, he didn't tell Daisie, but he also had hopes of seeing Joy). As usual, Daisie, the Plymouth Hill native, was right. First Alec had to spend the night at the airport. Then it took him an entire day, late into evening hours, to get home. The slick windy drive of three hundred miles took over sixteen hours, and nighttime felt even more treacherous. Once again, he saw cars turned off the road and stranded along the shoulders of the white-blanketed highway every few miles. His biggest fear was that they'd close the highway down. Daisie had warned him about that possibility too.

When he finally made it back to Plymouth Crest, he dropped his bags by the front door, hauled his body upstairs, and just plopped onto his bed.

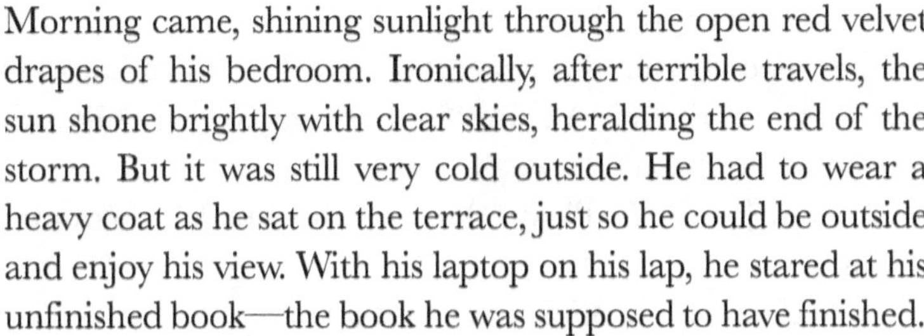

Morning came, shining sunlight through the open red velvet drapes of his bedroom. Ironically, after terrible travels, the sun shone brightly with clear skies, heralding the end of the storm. But it was still very cold outside. He had to wear a heavy coat as he sat on the terrace, just so he could be outside and enjoy his view. With his laptop on his lap, he stared at his unfinished book—the book he was supposed to have finished.

The air smelled of snow and maple trees. And the lake, far below, reflected golden, shining more sunrays than ever from an icy lake-mirror. Daisie told him the lake iced up every year. Only once or twice in her life had she not seen it freeze. Right now, it nearly blinded him with its reflected yellow light. It was as enchanting as the vista in the summer or the autumn leaves in fall.

He typed, not out of inspiration, but because he had to. All the while, birds rustled in the leaves fighting for his attention.

But it wasn't the sound of leaves rustling in the wind or squirrels climbing trees that finally stopped his fingers from moving. It was a far lovelier sound. Something that brought that feeling deep inside his chest again—that same feeling he'd first felt when he came to Plymouth Crest.

Joy.

Joy was humming. She was humming betwixt singing. It was her lovely singing voice, that same voice he had heard humming on the Fourth of July when he and Daisie were in need of a designated driver. She hummed and added words to that same tune, a song she had supposedly made up, but one she undoubtedly figured Alec would remember.

He stood up and, following her voice under the terrace, he saw his ghost. Joy stood barefoot in her coat staring at the lake with her hands in her pockets, squinting at the bright light, humming and singing. All the exhaustion from his trip left him.

"Joy!" he cried. "Joy!"

He leaned over the concrete ledge and cried out her name over and over. All she did was nod slowly while still gazing out at the lake.

"Wait, Joy. Wait. Please don't go this time! I'm coming down."

She didn't turn. But she nodded again.

He ran downstairs, nearly tripping over two steps at a time, and right out the front door. Then he rushed to the side of the house where he had seen her. He followed her voice. Finally turning the corner, he saw that same lovely profile, a face that had seemed to be imprinted in his mind during his whole journey to California: splashed on his passenger window, appearing in the window beside his seat in the airplane, on the windshield of his rental car in California. It was not Fifi's face, it was Joy's—those almond eyes with dark eyelashes, large red lips, and long flowing dark hair, staring at the icy lake, just as beautiful as Plymouth Crest itself. She had told him she created this vision for him. Her profile haunted him, just as that vision of his wife at the dining room table still haunted his memories. These pictures in his mind were more valuable than any photograph. And something about the fact that her face was Joy's, Josephine's creation created specifically *for him*, told him that she knew he was waiting for her.

"I love you."

That made her turn. But she looked confused.

"How did your trip go, Alec?"

"I still haven't finished my book. Maybe you could help me write the last chapter?"

"I'm not talking about your silly, dumb book," she said, shaking her head. "I'm asking about your daughter. How's her baby? Your grandson?" She forced a smile and squinted up at the sun. "That was so wonderful. I can't believe you went there through the terrible storm. There are two things I have always misunderstood about you. Your relationship with your family and your temper. I thought, being so like me, you didn't get along with your family. Seeing you battle the snow and sleet just to see your daughter's newborn baby was…amazing. I wanted to tell you that before I go. But as far as your anger problem…"

"Nobody's perfect."

"Yeah." She shrugged and smirked at him. "That's exactly what I was going to say. Nobody's perfect." She pointed her index finger at the sky, as if ticking an imaginary box. "There's something else about the two of us. I guess you can read my mind too."

"Please look at me, Joy."

"I really shouldn't," she shook her head. "Why haven't you gotten closer to your neighbor, Daisie? She's such a nice woman. I like her a lot. She would make a wonderful companion in your life."

"She's a witch."

"Nobody's perfect," Joy repeated with a laugh.

"I don't love her, Joy. I love you."

"How can you love someone who's dead? I'm like your book. I'm not real. Daisie's *real*. And she likes you. Or are you too dense to notice?"

"I noticed."

Alec touched her back, but her body recoiled from his touch.

"I… I can't, Alec. I can't… I told you. I have to go."

"Okay. Just know I love you so much. God, I'm going to miss you so much. I love your smile. Your energy. There's so much, you know, I love about you."

And she laughed.

"And I love your laughter."

She gestured back at the lake.

"When I first came here," she said, "I was looking for a place to start a new chapter in my life, just like you. Some stars get an island, or build themselves a castle, but I chose to live in the woods out in the middle of nowhere. Beside our awesome lake. Nobody understands how wonderful all this is to me, I think, except you. You and I."

"I love the view, just like I love you."

"Yeah? Well, stop saying that you love me already and go have a nice life."

He laughed. That made her laugh too.

"You really can't stay?"

"Are you crazy, Alec! You want someone who's not real to hang with you? I'm not real. Okay? You were right. I'm not real. Fifi died. I changed my look for you. This is all a fantasy, Alec. I'm not real. It's like…ghost makeup."

"I have no objections to you looking like Fifi, if you prefer. You can even look like that ghoul you once showed Daisie."

"I don't think you'd want me to look like that," Joy said with a chuckle.

Then they were caught staring into each other's eyes. It was that look of love.

Alec came closer. He noticed her breathing more softly. Then he ran his hand gently through her hair and she seemed lost in his eyes.

"If you must go," he said, "then…but if it's up to you, and you can stay, please don't go. You obviously haven't left yet."

"You have no idea what I'm missing," Joy said, breaking his gaze. She walked over to a tree, leaned against the trunk, folded her arms, and looked up at the clear sky. "When you die, Alec, there's this brilliant yellow light, and this amazing feeling of warmth and goodness that is so magnetic, and really the only thing, I think, that can keep you in this dreary, dark world is someone or something that haunts you. In my case, it was my hatred for Reggie. You know, I was never happy as a star, and when I finally found happiness, he ripped it from me. Now he could come back and hurt you."

"So you're here to protect me?"

"Of course. I would never want anything bad to happen to you. But I mean…no. I told you, when you die the only thing that can keep you from moving into that light is something that haunts you. Reggie haunted me first. I took care of him. Then there was…"

"Me."

"Yeah, you. But you have to think of your future, Alec. Think about Daisie, your good friend, or maybe someone else alive that is *real*. You know, someone who—"

"Joy," he said, coming closer again. He ran his hand through her long dark hair and over her soft cheek. He felt tears fall from his eyes. "You told me that we should be happy without thinking. You're thinking. You said we shouldn't worry, and, like the lake and the woods, enjoy the moment. You said this so many times. Why can't we enjoy our moments together? Even if it's only for a little while longer?"

Joy slowly shook her head.

"For a little longer?"

"I'm still here, Alec, aren't I?"

He embraced her so tightly over that. Then she touched her lips gently to his. And he kissed her soft lips harder. His hand ran through her long hair and he felt her arms around him, squeezing him.

"If you have to go, then go, Joy," Alec whispered. "But if you're thinking of my welfare, don't go for that. Because I don't want you to leave."

But then she started shaking in his arms.

"Why are you crying?" he whispered.

"You make me so happy, Alec. Yes, I love you. Yes. I

didn't think I'd ever meet a man in my life like you. I suppose I never did."

"So you'll stay?"

"Yes," she said, squeezing him tighter. "For you, Alec. Yes, I'll stay for you. I will."

"I will," Alec echoed, kissing her lips.

THE LAKE

ALEC SAT ON A PLASTIC CHAIR ON THE ROCKY AREA overlooking his lake. He had been coming down to the shore like this for so many years that he and Joy had finally just left chairs. It seemed it had become a tradition, when weather permitted, for him to walk down the hill every morning and write beside her. This morning, like so many times before, bright yellow light reflected off the water under a clear cerulean sky. And his ghost, as usual, sat by his side, wearing shades and sitting quietly, loving the view.

It was a warm autumn day with leaves turning that wonderful orange and brown. A perfect day, if it had not been for his hand shaking. That wasn't from the cold. His nerves were getting worse—that, along with a growing unsteadiness whenever he walked. When he had first arrived at Plymouth Crest, he could get to Daisie's place in less than an hour. Now, if he didn't drive, it could take two or three hours to make his way down the hill—despite Joy's help, supporting him along the way.

He glanced at Joy. The water reflected the sun's rays over her profile. For years now, she had worn her long hair white with blemishes on her perfect face and wrinkles on her skin. He never recalled asking her to do it, she just did it. But she never lost that whimsical, joyful countenance that he had fallen in love with. And she wore the same clothes—a dark shawl with jeans, without shoes, that she had worn when he saw her the first day he arrived at her house.

She seemed to notice she was being watched.

"You always have trouble finishing your books," she said.

"And you always help me finish them."

"But you really need to lay off the writing now, Alec. Or…stay inside the house. Your body's telling you to stop. You need rest."

"Never."

She reached over and put an arm around him, kissing his cheek. Then she just leaned her head on his shoulder.

"You know Danny is almost due for the birth of his granddaughter," Alec said. "He was hoping so much that I could come by and visit them in a few months, in Denver, around springtime. I thought—"

"No, Alec," she said, letting go of him. She shook her head. "I'd love for you to go, but you can't. You need to stay put in Plymouth Crest. This is what I'm talking about. You have to think of your health now."

"And I can't bring you along."

"Well, that too." She shrugged. "But you know I'll always be here when you get back."

And she always was. Joy always remained at Plymouth Crest, waiting for his return, every time he left: when Danny's daughter was born, when Danny had a son, and when Alec spent a month by his daughter's side before she passed away in California. Back home in Plymouth Crest, Joy stayed by his side at every birthday, at every meal, and during leisure time. She had been his constant companion for decades.

There was a white plastic chair, thrown on its side, now brown and dirtied from the passing of time, stuck in the rocks and sand behind Joy. That chair had once belonged to their friend Daisie, who had loved to spend time with them here by the lake years ago. All three of them had so many fun times together over the years. Daisie had passed away not long after his daughter, Rachel. But unlike at his daughter's death, Alec remembered fighting with Joy in a fit of mourning, demanding that she somehow magically bring Daisie back to stay with them as a ghost. He thought, if Joy could be back, why not his best friend? He couldn't imagine Plymouth Crest without Daisie. Daisie never returned.

But Joy never left his side.

"Why'd you stay with me all these years?" he asked. "How could you do that? Why didn't you leave, like Daisie did? You told me how much you wanted to go."

It was hardly the first time he had asked. She turned, removed her shades, and smiled.

"I love you."

"No, tell me," Alec said, shaking his head. "Don't just say you love me. You always say that."

"But I do love you, Alec," she said with a laugh. "That's why. I love you so very much."

"But you wanted to go. You said how beautiful it was on the other side. Why didn't you go?"

Joy looked down pensively. Then she laid a hand on his.

"Do you remember when we first met? You traveled to see your daughter in California when she gave birth to Danny. I'll never forget that. That was so amazing. I was going to leave, and I planned to go after Thanksgiving, but…I heard you talk to her on the phone. And then I saw you run to help her with her birth. For her. It made me think that you and I were missing something. Maybe life isn't just about the lake, or the trees, sun, clouds, Alec, or all the wonderful things we love so much in Plymouth Hill. Maybe it's about people. And I do love you. I love you so much. That's the reason, honest. I never loved any man more than you. You see, all this time you've thought your ghost, Josephine, had haunted you. That was one winter. You've haunted me ever since for the rest of your life."

He nodded pensively. But then, he shook his head.

"But you would never have heard me talk to Rachel if you had left after that Thanksgiving with Daisie. It wasn't just Rachel. It couldn't have been."

"No," she said with a nod. "It wasn't just that." She leaned over and kissed his white beard. "I already told you why. I kept being drawn to the light but… I love you, Alec. That's all. I don't know how else to put it. I wanted to spend more time with you. That's all."

He nodded.

"Thanks for letting me stay with you in your house all these years," Joy said.

And they laughed together. Alec remembered saying those exact words to her when he finally acknowledged she was a ghost.

But then Alec's hand tremored again. Then it burned. He grasped his fingers tightly, trying to stop the tremoring. He rubbed his shoulder, which had started to ache. He couldn't type. He couldn't hit any of the keys this morning.

All the while, Joy hummed. It was a different tune this time, one he had never heard. She did that, occasionally coming up with music in her head. Now she hummed and occasionally, quietly, sang words with the tune. It was a beautiful tune, as lovely as the view. And even though he wasn't feeling well, her voice soothed him. Did she know her singing soothed him? Her company soothed him so much too.

The pain came on sharper than ever. He struggled with a deep breath.

"Are you okay, babe?"

"No, I'm…having trouble breathing," he said, shaking his head. "I'm feeling that pain in my chest again."

His hand tremored more, not from nerves, but this time out of fear. And his fear seemed to only make his heart thump more crazily in his chest.

"It's okay," she whispered in his ear. "It'll be all right."

"I'm afraid, Joy. Do you think it's time?"

"Don't be afraid. Aren't you anxious when you travel, Alec? Is that nervousness or is it excitement? I'm excited. You're right, I've waited long enough."

"You're not afraid?"

"I am," she said, squeezing his hand. "I never saw what lies on the other side. I'm scared, for sure, but… I remember it being so tranquil, and I felt more at peace than I had ever felt in my life."

She took his shaky hand and brought it up to her lips, kissing it. Then she brought it down on his lap and played with his fingers. He stared at their hands together, something that had never before been possible.

"It is time," he repeated to himself with a nod.

Joy nodded back with her rueful smile. "I think so, Alec."

She helped him stand. Then she held him as they stood by the edge of the shore.

It seemed that the light shone brighter, not from the sun, not only over the trees and the water, but from every-where—from the air itself. And in a flash, Joy's features altered into Joy's younger face, which he remembered from when he first met her. Her long hair turned from white to black again. And her perfect face with almond eyes and perfect eyebrows, like her feet, had no blemishes. Both of them just stood before the brightest lake as yellow sunlight reflected off everything. It was not just the water that reflected the sun now. There was a yellow light glowing from the fall leaves, the autumn tree trunks and branches, even along the rocks on the wet sand at their feet.

They stood and waited. Then finally, hand in hand, they walked past the ledge and onto the water. But they didn't go in. They seemed to hover over it.

"I love this lake," Joy said.

"I love you, Joy."

"And I love you, Alec. Before I came back to stay with you, I caught a glimpse of this. Oh, I've been wanting to show you this for so long. I think waiting has been the hardest. You're right. But I wanted to wait just to show you and be with you. That's why I never left you. See, as much as this light attracts me, you attracted me more. Do you…feel it? Do you feel the light as it moves us towards it? Just wait. Oh, I think it's going to be wonderful."

"With you, Joy…it will be."

And he squeezed her hand tight. She squeezed his hand back, but as he turned to her, he couldn't see her anymore. The light blinded him too brightly. Yet all the while, he heard her humming her beautiful tune.

Then, as Alec felt the radiance surround him, he walked forward, while Joy held his hand.

THE END

ALSO BY A.L. HAWKE

PARANORMAL ROMANCE

- THE HAWTHORNE UNIVERSITY WITCH SERIES (I-III)
- THE HAWTHORNE UNIVERSITY WITCH SERIES (4-6)
- THE HAWTHORNE UNIVERSITY WITCH HOLIDAY COLLECTION
- SHADES
- PHANTOM MASQUERADE

- MY EVIL EYE
- THE GUARDIAN
- NECTAR OF AMBROSIA
- CORA

FANTASY: THE AZURE SERIES

- HARMONIA
- CORA: RISE OF THE FALLEN GODDESS
- AZURE BLUE
- CORAL RED
- PRINCESS SOJOURN

SCIENCE FICTION

- CANDY SAVANT SERIES

Books available at https://alhawke.com/books

PARTING WORDS

What did you think of *Haunting Joy*? By placing a book review, you can inform others of your thoughts and help spread the word about my book.

Want more? Periodically I like to send news regarding current or new projects. If you'd like to be privy, I encourage you to sign up to my email newsletter. Your information will remain private and you can cancel any time.

Sign up at www.alhawke.com or scan the following QR code:

ACKNOWLEDGMENTS

I want to thank my beta reader George B. for helping shape this book. Many scenes were revised and redrafted based on his input. And to my line editor, Stephanie Marshall Ward, for her polishing and character revision recommendations. To my proofreader, Alexa, for perfecting. And to Mirella Santana for her gorgeous cover art. Thanks for your help in creating a better book!

ABOUT THE AUTHOR

A.L. Hawke is the author of the bestselling Hawthorne University Witch series. The author lives in Southern California torching the midnight candle over lovers against a backdrop of machines, nymphs, magic, spice and mayhem. A.L. Hawke writes fantasy and romance spanning four thousand years, from pre-civilization to contemporary and beyond.

Visit A.L. Hawke at www.alhawke.com

Email: contact@alhawke.com

www.ingramcontent.com/pod-product-compliance
Lightning Source LLC
Chambersburg PA
CBHW032225190726

48289CB00007BA/2390